C000141524

FROM VIRGIN STREAM

A series of stories in verse covering most aspects of life. A roller coaster ride through human emotions, from birth to death and beyond.

Order through bookshops. Amazon internet bookshop U.K. and U.S.A. W.H. Smith internet bookshop U.K.

THE DREAM MAKER

A novel for teens and adults with an adventure into the murky past in the city of Leicester, England and fantasy dream trips to the field of Seetoos. The Land Of The Gabbering Gabbies and Planet Two Faced to meet some very strange creatures. This book also contains many topical subjects dealt with in a humorous manner.

Order through bookshops and Amazon internet bookshop.

The Sassenach from Ireland

With best wishes
from Robert Fallon

Robert Fallon

Matador
9 Priory Business Park,
Wistow Road, Kibworth Beauchamp,
Leicestershire. LE8 0RX
Tel: (+44) 116 279 2299
Fax: (+44) 116 279 2277
Email: books@troubador.co.uk
Web: www.troubador.co.uk/matador

ISBN 978 1780880 839

British Library Cataloguing in Publication Data.
A catalogue record for this book is available from the British Library.

Typeset in 11pt Palatino by Troubador Publishing Ltd, Leicester, UK
Printed and bound in the UK by TJ International, Padstow, Cornwall

Matador is an imprint of Troubador Publishing Ltd

To the memory of Bobby, my father,
and the literary legacy he left me.
To my dear friend Constance.
My sister Elizabeth.
Cousin Cherry
and
my cousin Bob Ross, a musician
in the Munich Philharmonic Orchestra,
German television personality
and recording artist.
Also a Conductor in his own right
with his international Brass Group
"BLECHSCHADEN".
Thank you all for your support
and interest in my literary pursuits.

CONTENTS

THE SASSENACH

Robert Martin Fallon was born on Christmas Day 1884. His grandparents emigrated from the County of Cork in Ireland, during the potato famine of the 1840s. The potato crops destroyed by blight, a fungoid parasite, were their main source of income and nourishment. Like many of their kind on the brink of starvation they left their beloved Emerald Isle for Liverpool, in England, many more set sail for America and beyond.

His parents Martin and Sarah were brought up in the large Irish community who had settled in Liverpool. After their marriage they moved to the Spa town of Buxton, by the river Wye, in the peak district of central England. The town was a well-known health and holiday resort for the rich and famous. Martin, a Tailor by trade, hoped to build up a successful career in the town. They settled at 35, West Street, in a row of cottages backing on to open countryside. It was an idyllic place to raise a family.

Over the next fifteen years the river Wye and the high moors that rose above the town provided the family with recreation, exploration and plenty of interests for them all. With five daughters and two sons to clothe, feed and educate from one income, the family lived from week to week, saving for a rainy day was out of the question. The family was of the Catholic faith, for financial reasons the two sons were educated at a free Protestant school near their home. This gave them an early insight and a balanced view of the religious divide of that time. It also toughened them up mentally against the prejudice they would face in the future. By growing up in a wholly English community both boys spoke with distinct English accents. This would cause them much trouble and hardship in the years ahead.

When Robert was twelve years of age tragedy struck the family. At the wedding reception of a workmate at a local Inn, Martin became involved in a brawl with some drunken gatecrashers, which turned into a violent confrontation. He fell on some broken glass a splinter of which pierced his head; he died of blood poisoning a few weeks later.

After the family had come to terms with their grief, Sarah a woman of strong moral fibre made a brave decision. With no source of income and living off the generosity of a few friends, she decided to uproot her family and move north.

After selling most of the family furniture, and items of no essential value, the family set off with their few remaining belongings piled on a small handcart. Sarah knew their chance to find employment lay in the Lancashire Cotton Mills. It was early spring and progress was slow, the handcart also served as a roof over their heads as the family huddled together for warmth on cold and stormy nights. For the younger children it was an adventure, for the two eldest daughters and their mother a worrying and degrading experience. After weeks on the road they reached their destination, the town of Oldham. After the pleasant surroundings of Buxton, the grim looking Cotton Mills was a cultural shock for them all.

The two eldest girls got employment at a Cotton Mill. The wages from fifteen years old Ruth and thirteen years old Mary enabled their mother to rent two rooms in a terraced house with a small kitchen and outside toilet. Although this raised a great burden off Sarah's shoulders the family were still in a desperate situation. Another worry for Sarah was the thought of having to split her family up. The meagre earnings of the two girls could not support them all. After many sleepless nights she decided for the benefit of them all she had no other choice.

A cousin, Joseph Gibb, lived in the County of Fife, in Scotland. The village of Kelty lay in the heart of the Scottish coal mining industry, across the Firth of Forth river from Edinburgh. Sarah contacted Joseph, he promised to find work and somewhere to live for her two sons if they could make their own way to Scotland. With a heavy heart Sarah gave her sons what little money she had and a rough guide for the long journey ahead of them. The lads left with only the clothes they wore, and some waterproof sheeting and a blanket each strapped to their backs. Their mother and sisters waved them a tearful goodbye from the end of the cobbled street until they were out of sight.

Twelve years old Robert and ten years old Joe, although of similar build, were like chalk and cheese in many other ways. Robert was mature for his age, spoke only when necessary and after much thought. Joe on the other hand was full of mischief, and would speak out without thinking of the consequences, which got him into some awkward situations. Their sense of adventure overcame their fear of the long journey ahead and it was comforting to know they had each other for company. They hoped to find odd jobs in exchange for food or money as they made their way north. They knew they would not starve, as it was early summer there was plenty of vegetables in the fields.

Five hours after leaving home, as they rested by a dirt track of a road, a Pedlar in his horse drawn cart, with three donkeys tied to the back, offered them a lift. He was a chubby little man with a red, weather beaten face, topped by a round wide brimmed hat. The canvas framed cart filled with goods was also his home. The lads spent two happy weeks with Jovial John, as he was known, helping to sell his wares in the small villages he traded in. They slept under his cart on their waterproof sheeting, well fed by the kindly Pedlar, wrapped warmly in their blankets against the cold night air. They also got many a free ladle of milk from the soft hearted milk women, who sold it door to door from churns pulled on tiny carts by small donkeys.

At the village of Waddington, near the Forest of Bowland, they parted from Jovial John. Having sold his wares and donkeys he was heading back to his base in Oldham. He took a letter from the lads to deliver to their family saying they were safe and well. The Pedlar drew them a route through the forest, which would take them past working sites where shelter and food could be found. Without the Pedlar's drawing they would have been lost in the maze of paths and cart tracks in Bowland Forest. They found work in a camp of tough axe wielding Foresters, doing odd jobs and carrying water supplies from a stream some distance away. They were fed and treated pretty well, but Joe earned himself a few cuffs around the ears for voicing his opinions, when being deaf and dumb would have been a much safer option.

After a week Robert decided to move on before the outspoken Joe got them into serious trouble. These rough living characters were not the type to fool around with. After leaving the Foresters they spent two rain soaked nights, sheltering under their waterproof sheeting, deep in the forest. It was with a great sense of relief on the next day that they sighted the dwellings of several Charcoal Burners. They received a warm welcome from the families who lived in a forest clearing in turf roofed huts. They cooked their food in large pots hanging from wood poles tied together at the top, in the shape of a pyramid, eating as a community in the open. An open sided shelter, made from branches with log seating, was used in bad weather and for social evenings.

The lads enjoyed the hospitality of Mary and Patrick Docherty, who were childless and eager for news of the outside world. The charcoal made from the wood provided them with a reasonable but isolated lifestyle. They, like many other Irish immigrants, had through necessity found refuge all over the British mainland. Many had settled in Scotland with their Celtic brothers, the Scots. After a few days of resting and being pampered the lads reluctantly moved on. After they had left the

Forest of Bowland behind them, the journey became much easier.

They got lifts from friendly Carriers who delivered mail and were the only public transport between small villages and distant towns. The horse-pulled carriages were not a comfortable way to travel on the rutted, dusty roads, but they gave the lads aching feet a welcome rest. As they reached the Scottish borders they stayed with Kevin Kellar and his wife Margaret. Kevin rented a number of rabbit warrens on the land of an estate owner. From these, and a vegetable crop tended by the buxom and motherly Margaret, the Warrener and his wife made a comfortable living selling their produce at a local market. For helping Kevin to catch and skin his rabbit catch, they were fed a rich diet of rabbit stew, dumplings and vegetables. When they took to the road again they were in high spirits and full of confidence about the future.

After many more memorable experiences they arrived in Edinburgh and sent news of their progress to their worried family back in Oldham. After the short ferry trip from Queensferry across the Firth of Forth river they were nearing the end of their long journey to the north. After a fifteen mile walk they reached the town of Dunfermline, the birth place of Andrew Carnegie, who became the town benefactor after making his vast fortune investing in railways and the oil industry, after he emigrated to America. They slept for the night in a wooden shelter in Dunfermline Glen, which now boasts a large statue of Andrew Carnegie at its entrance. After an early morning wash in a stream, they walked the last five miles to the small village of Kelty.

Joseph Gibb their mother's cousin had been waiting anxiously for their arrival. He and his wife Judith, three daughters and son, gave both the lads a warm welcome. The full story of their journey was listened to intently. They spent a week with the family sleeping in the small living room, before Joseph introduced them to the owner of their new lodgings. This left the two lads with a sense of foreboding.

Tam Bailey a widower, lived in a derelict shepherds cottage with an insane twenty years old daughter named Maggie. He was a heavily bearded man of stocky build, unwashed, with the distinct odour of the sheep he looked after oozing out of his pores, and from his ragged clothes. Joseph Gibb shrugged his shoulders in sympathy when the lads looked at him in dismay. Bailey had been Joseph's last resort, most of the villagers had large families to support and the lads at that moment had no source of income. Bailey would be content with a few pence now and then to drink himself into oblivion. The lads would soon find out that apart from his lack of hygiene Tam Bailey was not a problem, it was his mad daughter Maggie. Most of the time she was as sane as anybody was but her mind could blow at any time. This kept the lads in a state of unease whenever she was around. As there was only two bedrooms their sleeping quarters were the living room, on two camp beds that Joseph Gibb had borrowed. Washing was a cold experience in a large tub in the backyard. There was however plenty of coal for the living room fire.

Robert was anxious to start work to support himself and Joe and help out the rest of the family back in Oldham, but there was a slight problem. In 1876 a law had introduced compulsory education until the age of thirteen. After a week he got a job at the Aitken Colliery in Kelty and made excuses to avoid producing his birth certificate until he was thirteen. He started work in the ponies' stables down the coalmine. His Irish background, he mistakenly thought, would be to his advantage among the Scottish miners and their Irish immigrant workmates. Both races from historical events had no reason to like the English. With his distinct English accent and slight build he became an easy target for his adult workmates. He was singled out as the victim for many cruel pranks and more than a few beatings. Throughout the mine he became known as the Sassenach, in his case not a term of endearment.

Joe was facing the same problem at the Protestant school he

attended. His English accent, crazy as it may seem, was a bigger issue than his Catholic upbringing. For six months Robert the Sassenach took all the physical and mental abuse without a murmur of complaint. He knew that getting involved in arguments would only make matters worse and probably lose him his job. At last his patience snapped, he had the audacity to tell his chief tormentor to clear off and leave him alone. Jamie Black, a man who was feared for his strength and fiery temper, promptly picked up a shovel and broke it over his victim's back.

Off work, because of this incident, Robert and Joe had time to think and talk about their plight and decided what to do about it. Most of the coalminers, to escape from the grim reality of their lives, spent most of their leisure time either racing, or Hare Coursing their Greyhound and Whippet dogs in the miles of open countryside. Playing Pitch and Toss with pennies although this gambling activity was frowned upon by the authorities, a lookout would warn when any local constabulary were sighted. Probably the most popular form of recreation was downing whisky and beer chasers in Kelty and the surrounding village pubs in Lochgelly, Glencraig and Lochore.

The 'Auld Shank' tavern on the Ballingry to Loch Leven road, and some miles from the coal mining villages, was a popular retreat from reality.

In many respects Joseph Gibb stood out from the crowd, a teetotaller and amateur boxer, he coached the local youths in boxing, wrestling and running. His own son Rab would later become the founder member of a youth club in the village of Crossgates, where the road forked off to the nearby East coast and Largo. The birth place of Andrew Selkirk, better known as Robinson Crusoe, and the town of Dunfermline, in the inland direction. Joseph had kept a fatherly eye on the two lads but they had not burdened him with their problems, when they told him he offered to intervene on their behalf.

They refused saying, "Just help us get super fit so we can have a fighting chance when we face the thuggish ringleaders."

Joseph, who greatly admired the way his protégés had fended for themselves at such an early age, taught them the art of boxing and wrestling. He also set them a rigorous training programme. He was surprised by the quick reflexes and wrestling ability of them both. He also made sure they had at least three nourishing meals a week at his home. Tam Bailey's daughter, mad Maggie, cooked the food at their lodgings. This was a monotonous, though pretty nourishing diet of lamb stew from a large pot, which was continually topped up, jam sandwiches and an occasional bowl of porridge.

Mad Maggie had taken an instant dislike to Joe, his outspoken manner could send her over the edge and also bring out the spiteful side of her nature. Just the sight of Joe could send her into an ugly mood muttering to herself and shaking her fist at him in an angry tantrum. One day as the lads were by the tub in the backyard, having a wash, Maggie appeared from the front of the cottage ranting and raving that Joe had thrown a snowball at her. This resulted in her spitting in the stew pot to teach them a lesson. Robert who was interested in medical science told Joe not to worry,

"Let it boil for another twenty minutes or so and it will be all right to eat."

Two weeks later Robert woke up in the middle of the night with a screaming Maggie straddling Joe on his camp bed and beating the daylights out of him with her fists. He managed to drag her off the slightly battered Joe with some difficulty. From then on they kept the door jammed with a chair at night. Maggie would eventually be carted off to an Asylum, after running through the village in broad daylight ripping all her clothes off.

After Maggie's dramatic departure from the cottage life changed for the better for its two lodgers. Joseph Gibb's wife Judith, an attractive, pleasant woman in her mid thirties of Scottish and Irish descent, began to take a more active part in their lives. With the much feared Maggie gone, never to return, she visited the cottage for a few hours every week to make it fit to live in and collect their washing. She even managed to coax the drunken Bailey out of rags by buying him some second hand clothes. With her help Joe became master of the stew pot. She introduced him to a variety of cheap cuts of meat, including shin of beef, mutton, mince, brisket and pigs trotters. A regular intake of dairy products, porridge, fruit and home made bread also joined the menu.

After six months of Joseph's stamina building exercises, weight lifting and training in the martial arts, plus a healthy diet, both lads were in prime condition. Joe tested out his extra muscle power and newly attained boxing and wrestling skills in a two on one confrontation at school, surrounded by a circle of shouting youngsters. After handing out as much punishment as he took his more aggressive and persistent tormentors thought twice about upsetting him again. He even found that his English accent became less of a problem with his classmates of a more moderate nature. Robert the Sassenach was more than pleased with Joe's successful fight-back, but had the maturity to know that his own day of reckoning was some time off. He had avoided Jamie Black as much as he could; the rest of his workmates were beginning to show a little more respect. He suspected this was because his increased muscle bulk and their failure to make him show any emotion, apart from a steely eyed stare, was now making them feel a trifle uneasy.

He also kept his thoughts and activities as private as possible. This was unusual in the tight knit mining community, where everybody gossiped freely. By the age of fifteen he weighed ten stone of toned muscle and was making a name for himself as a Highland Games wrestler.

His situation came to a head when he started to work at the coalface with pick and shovel, earning top money. Jamie could no longer be avoided. On his first day at the coalface the workers sat having a short break to eat their snacks from vacuumed tins. These snacks were known as pit pieces and ranged in variety from pork dripping or cheese sandwiches to home made scones and clouted dumpling. When times were bad, and money was tight, jam or black treacle sandwiches staved off the hunger pangs.

Robert knew that Jamie Black was itching for a confrontation with him as Jamie shouted a string of insults at him from where he sat on the other side of the conveyor belt, with its load of coal they had just hacked from the coalface. Obviously news of the Sassenach's wrestling exploits were irritating him.

"Wrestle! You couldn't wrestle the skin off a black pudding you little English prick. One of these days I'm going to skin you alive."

The Sassenach was confident he could now take on and beat the sixteen stone Jamie as years of bad diet and drunken binges were beginning to show in his appearance and mobility. He was determined however, to confront Jamie without an audience, not one of his grinning workmates had ever shown him an ounce of sympathy. If reported to the mine manager for fighting underground he would lose his job.

A week later his chance came, he saw Jamie relieving himself in the empty pit pony stables and challenged him to a fight. Jamie stared at the Sassenach with a surprised look in his eyes, then a grim smile spread across his face as he chillingly declared,

"I'll gorge your eyes out you bloody little shit."

He did not get the chance to carry out his threat; his bull-like rushes were no match for the quick reflexes of his agile opponent.

He took the beating of his life unable to get to grips or land a blow. The Sassenach handed out his punishment in a clinical and brutal manner. A bleeding and exhausted Jamie Black accepted defeat in a neck breaking headlock. The fight however, had not gone unnoticed, a stable lad had watched the half hour beating in stunned silence, from the safety of an adjacent stable stall. The news spread like wildfire from the stables to the miners and surrounding areas. Jamie Black's three weeks absence from work, recovering from his wounds, added spice to the story as it was retold and exaggerated on. To give Black his due he later admired the young Sassenach for refusing to talk or brag about what had taken place, which saved him from further embarrassment. He became a keen follower of Robert and his brother Joe's wrestling bouts around the country. Joe had now left school and was working at the mine.

With them both now earning a wage they were able to rent a cottage for themselves, and their mother and two of their sisters who had moved from Oldham to live with them again as a family. Another sister stayed in Oldham having married a well-known local sportsman named Billy Ashworth. The two other girls emigrated to South Africa.

In the year 1906 a Japanese wrestler named Yokotani toured Scotland demonstrating the art of Jujitsu in exhibition bouts. Robert was amazed as he watched the little man, who weighed less than nine stone, immobilise a seventeen stone, very fit police Inspector in a matter of seconds. He also suffered the same fate when he had the honour as a promising young wrestler to face Yokotani in the ring. The friendly little Jap

Wrestling trophies

taught him later, the many pressure points that could disable opponents temporarily. This skill would play a very important part in his life. After the Jamie Black fight his reputation as a fighter and wrestler brought unwanted attention. He faced many no-holds-barred contests with young men intent on making a name for themselves. He also trained the County of Fife Constabulary in the art of self-defence.

By this time Joe was also an established wrestler and they toured the Highland Games wrestling circuit. In the following years they won many trophies and money prizes. Robert the Sassenach would become a Highland Game-wrestling champion and win the coveted silver buckled champion belt outright.

At Braemar Highland Games they met Anne Bathgate a pretty, young Highland dancer with a great sense of humour. Although Anne liked them both, Joe's forthright manner and cheeky grin won her over much to Robert's dismay. He was secretly madly in love with her, but as was his nature had not let his feelings show. A few months later Anne and Joe got engaged without telling her family. When her father Simon Bathgate, who owned a furniture shop in Dunfermline found out, he was not at all pleased.

Simon knew the brothers personally, having met them at many Highland gatherings. Joe's reputation as a womaniser was well

Silver buckled wrestling championship belt

known. His devil may care attitude to life; charm and physique made him a willing attraction to many of the opposite sex, married or single. Simon had another reason to be worried about their relationship. Three years earlier his only son John had a brief affair with a local girl then suddenly disappeared. Agnes, the girl in question also left the district some time later when her pregnancy became obvious. Ten months later Simon and his wife Margaret adopted a baby boy who was left on their doorstep. They named him John and he grew up to be a prominent sports personality, playing football for Dunfermline Athletic. His suspected parents were never heard from again, although some years on, a sighting of them was reported in far off Mexico. Anne built a strong bond with her adopted brother, or was it her nephew?

Simon Bathgate had always admired the man known as, 'the Sassenach' for his sporting ability and his quiet manner. He saw him as a much more suitable suitor for his daughter. Simon made sure that gossip about Joe's flirtations reached Anne in a steady flow from him and her friends. She finally broke off the engagement. After a time her parents encouraged her to invite Robert to the family home.

13

Diamond wedding anniversary: Robert Fallon and wife Anne

As time went by Anne warmed more and more to his companionship and reliable nature. Joe took the news of his brother seeing his former fiancé Anne, with no ill feelings saying with a grin,

"You no what brother, life is stranger than fiction."

They had always been there for each other, through good times and bad. The fact they had both fallen in love with the same girl only strengthened the bond between them. Shortly after, Joe met a Welsh girl and having scattered his wild oats near and far, got married and settled in Kelty. To the surprise of friends and foes alike he became a faithful and devoted husband.

After courting Anne for six months Robert asked her parents for their permission to marry her. He was surprised when they refused, saying she was too young with her eighteenth birthday two months away.

"Well when can I marry her?" he asked.

Unwilling to part with their only daughter at such an early age they declined to answer. This was when both men underestimated each other's stubbornness. Four months later

Robert, with Anne by his side, again asked for permission to wed. He was told,

"Not yet, maybe in a year or two."

To this he replied, "Well please yourselves but she is three months pregnant."

Simon Bathgate never forgave Robert the Sassenach for taking his daughter's virginity before marriage. To him it was the ultimate betrayal. Reluctantly, he gave them permission to wed. After the wedding Anne's contact with her family was limited to a few secret meetings with her mother and stepbrother John.

Anne and Robert rented a mining company cottage in Waverly Street, Lochore, a village not far from Kelty. He got a job at the nearby Mary Colliery as a Back Ripper. This job was well named only the strongest and fittest could manage it. Part of the work involved opening up new roadways and junctions, clearing rock falls with basic hand tools and where necessary supporting the roofs with pit props.

As well as being extremely dangerous it also meant working in cramped, dusty and sometimes waterlogged conditions.

Their home consisted of a small kitchen, two rooms with large bed recesses, which were curtained off, and a large attic. The living room contained a large black-leaded fire range with two built in side tanks to heat water. Anne gave birth to twenty children in this house but only thirteen survived into puberty. Bobby, the eldest of her three surviving sons told the following tale when his own family had grown up.

"When your grandfather put his arm around your grannie and said, Anne it's time you had a treat I am going to take you for a night out, you could bet your last penny that the midwife would be visiting nine months later."

Many of the miners could not read or write. Robert, with his soft English accent was a good speaker and by now highly respected. He was elected as a delegate of the National Union of Mineworkers. Through this he became a member of the

Parish Council and a close friend of Joe Westwood the Secretary of State for Scotland.

The two brothers volunteered for service in the armed forces during the First World War. Robert, a trained first-aid man had practiced his skill at many mine accidents. These included the amputation of a miner's arm, which was trapped under a huge rock when a roof caved in.

He served in the Royal Army Medical Corps on a hospital ship. At the battle of Gallipoli he treated many wounded including a friend from Lochore named Bill Kelly. He also recalled the sea full of bodies and the many injuries caused by barbed wire hidden in the shallow water where the troops waded ashore. When the hospital ship returned to Britain it was sunk in an explosion off Seaham Harbour, County Durham. The Sassenach survived and was fished out of the icy sea to spend two months in hospital and at home, recovering from pneumonia. He was then attached to the Argyll Regiment serving on the front line. He was taken prisoner when they advanced too far into the enemy defences and were surrounded, three months before the end of the war.

He returned home without any physical injury. Joe didn't have his brother's luck; he was badly gassed in the trenches in France. Although in a very weak state he insisted on carrying his kitbag through the streets on the homecoming victory parade. One week later he died from mustard gas poisoning. A grief stricken Robert returned to his work down the coalmine. For the next eight years he was still fighting but this time it was as a miners union official, for better pay and working conditions. This eventually led to the General Strike in 1926.

This long drawn out strike brought misery and dreadful hardship to the coalmining communities. The British government sent soldiers from a regiment known as the Black and Tans to the County of Fife. This regiment had a rather tarnished reputation in certain places, it was sent from a tour of duty in Ireland. There main duties were to guard the coalmines against any attempted sabotage by the miners, and stop desperate families searching for small pieces of coal amongst the dross in the huge mounds of coal waste. The local name for these mounds, which scarred the landscape over a large area, was coal Bings.

Late one night there was a loud hammering on Robert the Sassenach's door. He was alarmed to find a group of soldiers who asked to speak with him. Fearing he was about to be arrested for his miners union and welfare activities, he invited them into his home. The real reason for the visit took him by surprise. It appeared that through local gossip his wrestling and fighting ability had become the chief topic of conversation in the soldiers hastily erected wooden barracks, near the neighbouring village of Glencraig. They even knew about the time a drunk had insulted Joan one of his daughters. He had given the man a sound thrashing and held him out of an upstairs window of Lochore Institute by his feet, until he screamed an apology. That as a Parish Councillor his distribution of charity gifts to the community was more than fair, his own family on occasions went without. As a miners union official he had earned the respect of his workmates the hard way, at the coalface.

These men had not knocked then hammered on his door that night on a mere whim, they had spent a lot of time and effort planning what they were about to discuss with him.

They were on the verge of mutiny against their brutal and sadistic Sergeant Major, who was intent on making their lives a misery, mentally and physically. Would he, the Sassenach, be willing to take part in a no holds barred wrestling contest against their Sergeant Major? They had arranged for a substantial amount of money to be raised as prize money, on a winner take all basis. Everything necessary to stage the event would be supplied by them. Although he had been retired from the sporting scene for some time the Sassenach, a non-smoker and a teetotaller, still kept his body in good condition. After two days of thinking it over he decided to take up the challenge. He was hardly in a position to refuse his standing in the community was at stake. With his three sons also on strike the prize money, if he won, would be more than welcome. Also the soldiers were going to arrange other events to make it into a Gala day. This would help to raise the morale of the whole community.

The wrestling contest would take place at the top end of Waverly Street on a large open space, next to the Ballingry to Benarty Hill road. This barren area was used in better times for penny Pitch and Toss schools. It was also a meeting place for the women to barter and gossip, while their bairns played Paldy Beds and Marbles. Kate the Tinker was there every Sunday, selling second-hand clothes from her horse drawn cart. The clothes were said to come from a Sanatorium for the terminally ill near Kinross, on the other side of Loch Leven. Kate was also well known for her habit of standing over drains in ankle length loose dresses, with steam arising all around her.

On the day, the streets resounded to the sound of the Bagpipes and Drums of local bands, who added a refreshing splash of colour to the area, in their Highland attire. A large crowd from near and far mixed with the soldiers to watch preliminary bouts of boxing and wrestling, all eagerly waiting for the main event.

The Sassenach's eldest son Bobby took his place in the ring as his father's second. Young Bobby felt extremely worried, as he looked across the ring at his father's opponent. The six-foot, fifteen stone Sergeant Major and physical training instructor looked in excellent condition. Besides the cruelty in his icy stare, what made him even more scary was the hairiest chest Bobby had ever seen on a man. As they waited for the bell to start the bout the Sassenach whispered to his son,

"Bobby, I will have to finish this quickly this man means to do me serious harm."

At the sound of the bell Robert the Sassenach shot across the ring before his opponent had time to move. Grabbing two fistfuls of the Sergeant's hair on his chest, he twisted his clenched fists with all the strength he could muster. Twisting his body as he dropped on one knee he got his shoulder under the Sergeant's midriff and pulled the man downwards. He now had the shoulder leverage to force the man's legs upright, with his head at an awkward angle to the floor. The Sergeant Major with his neck and spine in jeopardy and screaming in agony had no alternative but to submit. It was a moment to savour for soldiers and locals alike as a beaming Sassenach raised two fistfuls of hair in triumph.

Later in life Robert and Anne moved to a new housing estate beneath the slopes of Benarty Hill, in Ballingry. On the other side of Benarty Hill lies Loch Leven, where Mary Queen of Scots was imprisoned in its Island Castle.

Robert the Sassenach died peacefully aged seventy-eight. The love of his life Anne lived in Ballingry until she died aged ninety-one. Ballingry cemetery was their final reunion.

As grandson and namesake of Robert the Sassenach I am the proud owner of his wrestling championship belt and his First World War service medals.

The Sassenach's wrestling trophies, war medals, silver watch chain and Royal Army Medical Corps silver and gold medal for being 1915 wrestling champion

My grandfather's life and mine are linked by a number of strange coincidences. We were both active sportsmen. He lived in Scotland from the age of twelve.

I left Scotland to live in England at the same age. We both had a hard time because of our accents, his problem I hasten to add, much more serious than mine. He overcame his problem through boxing and wrestling; I gained respect as a small, hard tackling Scrum-Half on school rugby playing fields. We both joined the Armed Forces. I also visited my future wife's parents in exactly the same circumstances as he did. To top it all my great grandfather was a Tailor; I finished up spending most of my working life producing garments in the Hosiery trade.

People say that if they had their life to live over again, they would live it differently. I think this is a delusion. Our genes and circumstances determine who and what we are.

THE AULD SHANK

It stands by
Loch Leven road
Many a tale
Pub: walls been told
From days of sawdust
And spittoon
When clothed capped miners
Drank till full.
Blue scars on faces
Stood out stark
From coal dust in cuts
As seam they hacked.
Pick and shovelling
Ten-hour shifts
'Auld shank' their pleasure
From back breaking pit.
Pitch and toss
Watch pennies spin
As with mates
Joke and drink.
Whisky glass turned
Upside down
A challenge to a fight,
Only fists they did use
Their code of honour
Now grimy news.

JAM JARS OF HOT TEA

Coal fire burning bright
Tin bath on fire rug ready
Waiting on Gran's miner sons
My uncles Sam and Jimmy.
On black leaded hob
Two jam jars of hot tea
Best china kept for Sundays
That's how it used to be.
Who would win the race
To step into hot bath
Then with a grin
leave water black
The loser's lot to have,
Uncle Sam the winner
Gulps his jar of tea
To clear his throat of coal dust
Gargles with great glee.
Pit siren gives its mournful wail
Of disaster down coalmine
Jimmy's jar of tea
Shudders on, the black-leaded hob
And with a crash falls to the floor
With no one near to touch.
Granny's face goes white and tense
Somehow she fears the worst.
Sam no longer wears a grin
He wearily gets dressed
Pit clothes he puts in bath to soak
The race was now no jest.
All have now left Planet Earth
Somewhere they wait for me
On Granny's hob I know there sits
My jam jar of hot tea.

BOBBY AND FAMILY

Bobby was the eldest of Robert the Sassenach's three sons. Like their father, they also became coal miners. They did not have much choice; it was the only notable industry in the county, known as The Kingdom of Fife, apart from the Linoleum factories in Kirkcaldy on the East Coast. None of the brothers inherited the sporting genes of their father, or their Uncle Joe. Bobby however, became interested in medicines and medical treatments like his dad. He attended instruction classes in first aid and became a first aid man at the Mary Colliery in Lochore, for a few pence on top of his wages. He treated many miners' injuries at the scene of the accidents underground. He recalled an incident when a miner was scalped in a conveyer belt accident. It was beyond his ability to do anything but to try and stem the bleeding, and comfort the man until doctor Sinclair arrived down the mine. When the doctor lifted the man's scalp to clean out the coal dust, skin and tissue debris, Bobby fainted.

The son aged 15

When he came round he helped the doctor to stitch the man's scalp back on. The miner was conscious throughout his ordeal and fully recovered. Grateful to a worried Bobby he promised never to reveal to anyone about his embarrassing blackout.

Bobby married his one and only sweetheart Lizzie Sparling, who he met at the Bethany Hall Baptist Church, in Lochore. She was six years older than twenty years old Bobby and the dominant partner in the marriage. They had four children in four and a half years, three daughters then a son. Many years later Lizzie told the family that after the birth of her son she more or less shut up shop sexually, the thought of having a yearly production line of children like her mother-in-law gave her nightmares. She also ran the family affairs including the chastising of the children most of the time. Her opinion on Bobby was that he was too easy going for his own good. As he did not down pints of beer with whisky chasers in the local Garries and the Goth pubs, smoke or gamble, her husband's life was pretty much family and Church related.

Even the families Sunday Church going and Saturday tea meetings where the children looked forward to a couple of sugar-coated buns came to an abrupt stop.

Bobby bought a number of utensils to make sweets, which were rationed at one pound a month per person. His homemade sweets became popular with neighbours, friends and relations. A Mr. Furthringham, an elder of the Church reported him to the tax authorities for running a commercial venture. Not the sort of behaviour you would expect from a devout Christian but there again Mr. Furthringham was possessed by the burning fires of hell and eternal damnation that he preached.

Robbie, the five years old son, still liked going to the Sunday school where he enjoyed the singing if not the preaching. Turning up at the Church one Sunday nearer the end of the service than the beginning, left him with a rather cynical opinion of preachers. When he entered the hall the

24

whole congregation turned round and stared at him with stern looks of disapproval. The preacher's eyes narrowed as he stared down at him from the pulpit and his forehead began to look like a furrowed field. Robbie looked at them in dismay, turned tail and ran like hell, and the devil himself was chasing him the thought running through his mind, why did they sing every Sunday the song that started with the words. - 'I always go to the Sunday school although sometimes I am late and though my friends laugh at me and say that I'm a fool but whether I know I'm going to go to the Sunday school, when they didn't really mean it?' Robbie's Church days were over.

Lizzie started to enjoy occasional nights out with her sister-in-law Annie Sparling who was married to her brother Birrel. Lizzie was also from a large family of thirteen children. They would treat themselves to an ice cream sundae, at Mazzonis ice cream parlour, in nearby Lochgelly and a visit to the Star cinema, or as it was also known, The Flea-Pit, in Crosshill, which was close to home. Bobby would be left with the kids and let them run wild.

At bedtime he would frighten the life out of them with a white sheet over his head, with a torch shining underneath, while wailing his head off. Lizzie always wondered why the kids encouraged her to have a night out.

When Robbie was just turned six Bobby was working at the coalface with a pick and shovel, when the roof collapsed; he was trapped for two days. As there were no ambulances available at the time he was brought the quarter of a mile home in a horse drawn coal cart with a broken leg and several other injuries. The family home at 5 Ivanhoe Avenue, the semi detached bungalow they rented from the coalmine owners, had only two bedrooms but the living room with its black-leaded fireplace was a decent size, as was the kitchen.

Its most pleasing feature was the bathroom with running water on tap and an inside-flushing toilet. They had moved into the newly built bungalow three years earlier from an old semi detached cottage, just off the main street, behind Dick's the bakers and the accumulator shop, which recharged the batteries for the wireless. Bobby was unable to work for two months as he recovered from his injuries. With no money coming in times were hard. The girls were very unhappy, as clothes were cut up and re-stitched together and changed hands from Lizzie to daughters. Bobby could have made a few pence making sweets but he was well aware that the taxman and the Church were keeping a watchful eye.

Lizzie decided that it was time her husband tried to better himself. After studying at night school Bobby became a mining official known as a Deputy on a steady wage. It was a responsible job in charge of the Shot Firers who bored holes into the coalface, and placed in them the explosive charges, blasting the solid mass into manageable lumps.

In 1946 Lizzie talked her husband into moving South, to Ollerton Colliery in Nottinghamshire in England, for a better future for the family. There were few jobs in the Fife area for her daughters and the prospect, if they stayed put, of a working life underground for her son. It was two years before she and her family joined Bobby in England.

The next door neighbour's son Peter Richardson became manager of a coalmine in Leicestershire and Bobby became one of his staff. There was a suspicion that the easy going Bobby was in no hurry to find a house and resume the full responsibilities of married life. In Scotland, Lizzie, unlike most of the miners wives, always received an unopened wage packet from which she gave her husband a little pocket money each week. In England she had no idea what he was really earning but he did send her a substantial amount after paying for his lodgings, basic and recreational needs.

The family moved to the village of Griffydam about a mile and a half from the coalmine in Newbold Glory. The journey South, in an old furniture van, was far from enjoyable. The son and his dad sat in the front, with the pipe-smoking ageing driver, with engine and exhaust fumes seeping into the cabin through a hole in the floor. The rest of the family sat in a cramped space in the back with Roy the family dog, and a bucket for emergencies. The teenage daughters and twelve years old Robbie, although sorry to leave friends and relations, were excited about the move, as their parents had explained the advantages. Robbie and his cousin Alec Sparling had been close pals since they were toddlers. Alec was so upset about them going to stay in England he refused to see them off. Robbie would also miss his chum and Auntie Annie's homemade cakes and scones. His own mother was not into the making of the tastier things in the kitchen.

Unable to view the property beforehand Lizzie, on her husband's recommendation, had agreed to take out a mortgage on their new home but was dismayed with what she saw. It was situated on the corner of a main road, and the road into the village at the bottom of a steep hill, a more dangerous site would have been very hard to find. The house itself was spacious but badly in need of redecorating, the biggest shock was in a little shed at the bottom of the garden. It housed a large metal bin boxed in with a large hole in the solid wooden top. They had moved to what they imagined would be utopia to a house in need of renovation with the only toilet facility a dry loo, which was only emptied once a fortnight.

First impressions gained Bobby a tongue lashing from Lizzie, and many sulky looks from the rest of the family, and future discoveries would not help to quell family resentment. When Lizzie and the two eldest girls Elizabeth and Ann found work in the nearest town of Coalville, and Milly and Robbie attended Broomleys school, the outside loo was used as little as possible.

They were welcomed to England by the widow Mrs. Griffin who was Bobby's landlady in her tiny cottage, a few yards up the road leading into the village. The dear old soul had gone to the trouble of making tea and porridge to welcome them. She was a little woman and a bit of a character, a regular pints of

Guinness drinker at the Wagon and Horses public house, directly across the main road from the Fallons new residence. She had a large bulbous nose that looked like it had been sprayed with airgun pellets, a regular use of snuff had produced a permanent yellow stain from nostrils to upper lip. She also had a habit of letting rip with loud bursts of wind and carry on talking without any sign of embarrassment.

After they got settled into their new home the family, as a whole, got busy redecorating the house. When stripping the wallpaper off the third bedroom they discovered a door, which was papered over. The excitement at what they might find turned to dismay; it was a fourth bedroom with a gaping hole in the ceiling and roof. There was also an old wine cellar where the tiled floor had been smashed up and a lot of digging had been done. According to Mrs. Griffin, the previous short-term owner of the house became convinced, from years of village gossip, that a fortune in savings was buried in the cellar, but his hard labour brought him no reward.

The move to England had a harmful effect on young Robbie's education, used to strict some might say, brutal discipline at school in Scotland he took the wrong attitude to the more relaxed and humane education system in England, going as far as to play truant now and then. Being a target for bullying because his accent made him a target for curiosity didn't help, his only outlet for his frustration was on the rugby field or to miss school, he was lucky that he avoided any serious trouble.

Two years later they were all on the move again. After a family discussion a mortgage was taken out on a newly built semi-detached house with all mod cons and large gardens front and rear. It was in a village four miles from Leicester City centre. The girls were really pleased finding well-paid jobs in the city, which also improved their social lives. Bobby however, because of transport problems, had to move to Ellistown Colliery, which was two miles off the main bus route. Apart from odd lifts from other miners he often faced a two-mile walk to and from his work. Shortly after their first move from Scotland to Griffydam the family dog was hit by a car outside their house. With both its front paws broken the vet said it would have to be put out of its misery. Robbie was really upset when he left without it from the vets. The vet must have been touched by the state the lad was in and he turned up at the family home two weeks later with the dog, both its front paws were in plaster. The kindly man refused to take any payment.

The next house move to Groby was a fatal one for fox terrier Roy. The second eldest daughter Ann, rushing off to work one morning left the front door ajar, this house was also near a main road, and Roy chasing after her was run over by a bus. Roy was buried in the back garden with a few tears. This put Robbie off having pets again. He had also got annoyed when a pet rabbit he bought, died a few days after he bought it and he had to give Malcolm Davies a bloody nose before he got his money back. He did change his mind some years later and have a few girlfriends and a wife, if pets are the right description that also gave him his fair share of joy and grief.

ELIZABETH

Shortly after the family moved to Groby, Elizabeth took a bad fall while out horse riding, no bones were broken but she was badly bruised and shaken up. This coincided with a loss of weight and she developed Tuberculosis, she became seriously ill and spent the best part of five years in a sanatorium at Markfield in Leicestershire. At that time the treatment appeared to be plenty of fresh air.

This included the glass patio doors in the wards being left wide open in the winter. Elizabeth would be nice and cosy in bed,

surrounded by hot water bottles, while her visitors shivered in their winter woollies. Today a regular dose of pills would have cured her condition without the need of hospitalisation. In the end she was operated on, her back opened up and packs put in both lungs. Very few people survived this operation; she was told it would be unwise to get married, and having children was out of the question if she recovered from the operation.

With the help of her strong will to live she survived and was moved to a convalescent home in Norfolk. She and her two sisters were completely different in looks and personality but none of them had a problem attracting the opposite sex. Elizabeth's boyfriend, who had been with her throughout her illness, travelled to Norfolk every weekend no matter how bad the weather, on his 350cc Royal Enfield motorbike.

After she had fully recovered Derek proposed to her and the wedding day was set, which led to a surprise visit to his future parents-in-law's home, by his father and stepmother. They wanted Elizabeth's parents to use their influence to stop the wedding, as it would not be fair to Derek, who would finish up looking after an invalid. The wedding went ahead and the marriage survived all the doubts and anxiety, Elizabeth gave birth to a healthy baby girl and later a boy. She worked most of her married life for The British Gas Board until retirement age. In later years she nursed a very sick Derek until the strain took its toll on her own health and she could no longer cope. Approaching eighty years of age she still enjoys short trips in her automatic car, arthritis put a stop to driving a manual one. All the female side of the family suffered in varying degrees from arthritis inherited from the Sparling side of the family and jokingly referred to as the Sparling curse. After much persuasion from her doctor Elizabeth bares her stitched up back to puzzled medical students on their examinations study groups. Derek is now quite content in an excellent care home with visits from his children, grandchildren, wife and friends.

ANN

She was the second eldest of the three sisters, and more reserved by nature, her boyfriend of three years was posted abroad on his National Service of two years. Ann stayed faithful to him and rarely went out to socialise. Near the end of his time in uniform boyfriend Tony wrote to her saying he had met, and formed a relationship, with another girl. Ann decided to get out and about to enjoy herself. When Tony got demobbed he wanted to renew the courtship, Ann refused his offer. She eventually married an American airman Frank Bowley, like her mother she had four children in a short space of time. Frank's service career ended through heart problems. Although on a good forces pension he got bored after a while and opened a nightclub one hundred and fifty miles from the family home in Florida, with Ann doing the accounts from home.

After a worrying start from picketing and sabotage by a religious group 'The Peek-a-Boo' club became a very

successful business venture. Their lives began to unwind, when Frank started staying at the club through, so he said, pressure of work. With many of the girls they employed more than pleasant to look at and with outgoing personalities, Ann's suspicions were aroused. After making a few discreet enquiries, she found out that the manageress of the nightclub was also Frank's mistress. In the early hours one morning she drove to the club and then to the home of the manageress, Frank's car was in the driveway. She did not confront them; instead she left her car, with the keys in, and drove back home in Frank's car using the spare set of keys. She said the agitated state he was in when he got home was some consolation for his betrayal, but he wanted the best of two lifestyles, torn between two women with completely different personalities. Ann refused to get involved in a three party relationship and insisted he left the family home.

History repeated itself when once again Ann decided to let her hair down and socialise more frequently. She took up ballroom dancing on a semi-professional level, with a handsome young dancer named Bill.

They became quite successful on the dance floor and Ann's house held its share of dancing trophies and photos in glamorous dresses. For some reason this annoyed Frank, who supported the family financially and visited the house frequently. Ann's friendship with Bill was purely platonic but Frank, as he deserved, was kept in the dark about this. She did have several romantic affairs but never applied for a divorce, neither did Frank. This was a constant annoyance to his mistress, it meant in family and business affairs she took a degrading understudy role to his wife. When her dancing partner Bill got married, Bill, his wife and Ann opened a ballroom dancing club, as a joint venture not far from husband Frank's nightclub in Bradenton, Florida.

Eventually Frank had major surgery on his heart to replace a faulty valve, this involved breaking his ribs. Ann was at his bedside almost constantly until he recovered. He said the after effect was as if he had been kicked in the chest by a horse. Years later when he was in his fifties the same operation was again needed if he was to survive. He refused to go through the ordeal and died. He had invested in many ventures including another nightclub, this left his wife, family and mistress financially secure, and his two sons Don and Dean were to enjoy the legacy of a nightclub each.

Ann is still alive and content with her dancing club activities and the company of her children and many grandchildren. Her eldest son Don, I am sad to say died suddenly in his forties and is sorely missed.

MILLY

The youngest daughter fell head over heels in love with a handsome hunk who was a prominent amateur rugby player. The only unkind thing one can say about Ken the strapping athlete, was he also suffered from athlete's feet. The last place

you would want to be was in the same room as Ken when he took his shoes and socks off. The marriage only lasted a short time and as Milly was known to have said some years later to her brother's sister-in-law, there were faults on both sides.

Ken's abiding passion was rugby, he also did well in business as an executive in a wholesale grocery concern. He was at one time the President of a well-known rugby club in Leicester. Milly, like her sisters was an attractive young lady and soon became the target for the amorous advances of another replica of a leading man in many love stories and films. Ernest, a tall dark and handsome area manager of a large Hoover machine company with an even larger expense account. The only trouble was as Milly found later to her dismay; Ernest was a married man. Milly went to live with sister Ann in Florida with the idea of making a new start in life. Ernest, to give him credit, was persistent and had kept in touch with her. After two years in America he lured her back with the promise of getting a divorce and marrying her. After a romantic reunion Ernest kept stalling about his divorce and was seen by some of Milly's friends having a romantic dinner in a Leicester restaurant with a pretty young blonde lady, when he was supposed to be in Northampton. This was the last straw as far as Milly was concerned; she cut all ties with the smooth talking Ernest.

A year later she was introduced to Michael a divorcee with two children, he would turn out to be her partner for the rest of her life. They were married soon after meeting. When Millie came back from America she stayed with her brother and his wife and children for some time before taking out a mortgage on a house in Vernon road, Leicester, a stones throw from Grace Road the home of Leicestershire cricket. She sold the house at a handsome profit and with Michael invested the money in a recycled parts business for the car industry; at one time they employed thirty people.

When they retired they became known to family and friends as the Gypsies, they spent months over many years touring America in a caravan. Milly finished up with more than her fair share of the Sparling curse becoming part robot with artificial hips and knees. These she treats as minor ailments as well as her arthritic problems in neck and spine.

They have however, cut down their caravan trips to three months touring in Europe in the summer, and winter weekends with the caravan club in Britain.

I would like to add that apart from only being of average height, not extremely handsome and his feet being in perfect condition, Michael has all the attributes that Milly yearned for in a husband. He is caring and attentive to her needs an excellent cook and they share the same interests. Especially, and not to be sneezed at, an obsession with hygiene. Also, continually buying new furniture and redecorating, a number of charity shops have a lot to thank them for. Mick as I call him, is a most agreeable and helpful chap to have as a brother-in-law and Milly was lucky to fall into such capable hands. He also has the most perfect set of his own teeth that I have ever seen in a wrinkly. Milly was nicknamed the Duchess by Bobby her father, when she visited him after he became a widower, he would have panic attacks and tidy up the house interior before she arrived.

Bobby's wife Elizabeth had suffered severe hip pain for many years, this was before joint replacement became an everyday occurrence, for years the house had been subject to the smell of pain killing ointments. By the time Lizzie had a hip replacement she was a frail old lady and more or less bedridden. Bobby had been retired for many years and did all the housekeeping and shopping. Lizzie at this time still had her wits about her and propped up on pillows in bed, would check the change from the shopping to make sure it was correct. Gradually her mind began to lose focus and she also became incontinent. Bobby with help from the family coped as best he could.

One Saturday afternoon I received a phone call telling me my father was ill and I should go and see him as soon as possible. When I got to his house an hour later the visitors who had alerted me had gone. I was shocked by what I saw. Father was lying in bed on his back his body shaking like mad as if he was having a fit, mother was lying beside him saying repeatedly,

"Behave yourself Bobby and stop all that moving about."

I phoned for an ambulance, which arrived with a crew of two; they studied the patient from a distance, had a whispering conversation between themselves, and then came to a startling conclusion.

"We are pretty certain your father is suffering from severe constipation the best thing for you to do is to phone for your doctor."

Having given their expert opinion they then left. When the doctor arrived he did a quick examination of the severely shaking Bobby and phoned the hospital telling them to send an ambulance as soon as possible and have a bed ready for the patient. Father's gall bladder had burst. The same ambulance crew came back to take him, far from being embarrassed one of them stated,

"It's a good job we told you to phone for the doctor it is the only way he will get immediate treatment and a bed."

I then asked the doctor about hospital accommodation for mother, "That is out of the question at such short notice," he replied.

I was getting angrier by the minute and said to him, "If that is the case doctor I am going to leave my mother on her own and hold you responsible for whatever happens to her."

After he made a number of phone calls the much needed hospital bed was found. Mother, who really needed to be placed in a geriatric ward, was placed in a short stay ward at Glenfield hospital on the outskirts of the city. Father was successfully operated on and recuperating at Leicester Royal Infirmary. A week later on a visit to mother she was fast asleep and looking dreadful, I told the family to expect the worst. The next day I went to see her again, and could hardly believe my eyes, she was sitting in a chair by her bed, her hair had been washed and permed and her eyes had a sparkle in them. I asked her how she felt and she complained of stomach pains, which I reported to the duty nurse who made an entry in the report book. Five minutes later a smiling young doctor came into the ward and shook me by the hand.

"Mr. Fallon, you are just the man I wanted to see your mother is feeling fine, just look at her she is ready to go home now."

He then went to mother clasped her hands, and with his nose almost touching her's, looked into her eyes in order to get her full attention.

"You are feeling great aren't you Lizzie? And you want to go home don't you?"

She nodded her head excitedly and said, "Yes! Yes!"

The doctor then came over to me with a smile of smug satisfaction on his face. "What did I tell you sir, you must feel really pleased and relieved."

"No, I am not bloody pleased or relieved, you try standing a few feet from her and she will not understand a word you are saying, besides, ten minutes ago she was complaining of stomach pains and it is in the report book."

He looked a bit sheepish as he said, "Let's have a look at the report."

He spent some time studying it as he thought of a way out of the awkward situation he was in. "Look sir, I know your mother is not in the best of health but she should not be in a short stay hospital. She should be in a geriatric ward, the only way I can get her in one is if you sign a form to say she is only going in for rehabilitation."

As there seemed to be no other way out of the situation I reluctantly signed the form. Mother was transferred to a geriatric ward at Leicester General Hospital the next day.

Meanwhile, father was recovering from his operation in the Royal Infirmary, fearful of leaving and having to look after his wife again. I waited two days before I visited my mother after her move, to give her a chance to settle. I have never felt so angry in my life when I entered the ward to see the frail body of my mother, being supported with her arms around the shoulders of two female nurses, being walked down the ward with her feet dragging behind her.

"What the hell do you think you are doing?" I shouted at the startled nurses.

"Sorry sir, but Mrs Fallon is in for rehabilitation and as such we must exercise her daily."

It was unbelievable these were two nurses in what is supposed to be a caring profession.

"And what about common decency and respect, can't you see my mother is dying?"

After being spoon fed with baby food by myself and members of the family for the following two weeks, mother was dead.

As reports through newspapers and the media in 2011

indicated, things have probably got worse instead of better over the past decades. It is irrational that in a country, whose morality as well as its finances are now bankrupt, that its citizens should have to leave its shores to enjoy a dignified ending to their lives.

My father recovered from his near brush with death, and free from his round the clock nursing duties, made the most of the years he had left. At the age of eighty-six he wrote the family tree on which the first two stories in this book are based. He died peacefully and with dignity at the age of ninety-two from heart failure.

Bobby, Lizzie and family

THE PREACHERS

They come in different disguises
To enlighten, frighten and chastise
Read out Gospel from religious book.
Some speak of Brimstone and Damnation
Others of Virgins in waiting.
Wise words written for our good
Used on weak willed by the scheming.
A few in expensive business suits
With flashy wives, mansions build
Bought with money from converts
A couple in prison now domiciled.
For sexual perversions others go down
With blind eyes turned by their peers.
Some against equality of the sexes
Think only men can reach our senses.
Others with power gone to head
Think are Immortal one on earth.
A lot of good some of them do
But safer to read and think for self.

1941 – THE TAWSE

In Scottish schools
It reigned supreme
For many generations
Of leather made
Two inches wide
The hand and wrist
With might did find.
Cut into strips
Giving much pain
Red weal's of discipline
Was tawse's aim.
Five years old
A tiny mite
In front of class
He stood
For peeing against
The wall of school
Was now about
To pay in full.
The Tawse came down
Six times in all
Made hand swell
He wanted to bawl
But with his pride
Now at stake
Unflinching he stared ahead.
The Tawse was
Law and order
Teachers with parents
In control
Of offsprings who
Stepped out of line
Made to do
As they were told.

D-DAY
June 6th 1944

From British Isles this day would die
Proud young men for freedoms cry.
To vanquish tyranny of Nazi Heil,
As Europe it raped, enslaved, defiled.
The allies did Germans much confuse
In dummy bases, machines and news,
With backup strong the Nazis scanned
Beaches not in battle plan.
Then allied forces made history
Crossed English Channel on this, D-Day.

The sky was filled with drone and shapes
Of airborne armada with much at stake,
Towing large gliders filled with men
To glide inland, disrupt, defend.
The sea alive with ships enmasse
Some floating harbours towing aft
A fuel line under sea
Would sustain attack into Germany.
From Normandy beaches troops stormed ashore
To fight the Nazis to poisoned core.

Many years have gone on by
Their deeds of valour will never die.
The suffering for us was not in vain
We bow our heads, freedom still reigns.
Remember we will the debt that's due
Till unto death we join with you.

V.E. DAY
1945

Church bells rang
Gave out the news
Victory was ours
In World War Two.
The nation poured
Into the streets
With hugs and cheers
Tears of relief.
At last we're free
Of Nazi Heil
Bombs, bullets, torture
Gas chambers file.
Streets were turned
From drab to gay
With Union Jacks
On proud display.
Tables laid out
For a feast
Ration books emptied
Supplied the eats.
Okie koky, Lambeth walk
Singing, dancing as rejoiced
Blackout over, street lights on,
Starting of
A bright new dawn.
The world owes much
To bulldog breed
We gave our best
Freedom to keep.

NATIONAL SERVICE

In the nineteen fifties conscription was a major topic of conversation in the lives of British youth and young men. As an apprentice learning a trade you could be exempted until you were twenty-one, if not, eighteen was the call up age. It was also possible to sign on as a regular at seventeen, for a minimum period of three years. Many took this option for the small amount of extra pay, or to get away from lousy jobs and such. This also gave you the slim chance of joining the Royal Navy or the Royal Air Force and avoid the possibility of being a front line soldier. As usual Great Britain had its nose stuck in trouble spots all over the globe, still trying as it is today, to stay a Super Power. The truth was that Britain was virtually bankrupt, its resources drained by the Second World War. It would be paying off huge war debts to America for the next fifty odd years. This was ironic to say the least. It was Great Britain who fought on alone after the rest of Europe had fallen to Hitler and his ally Italy. Without British resistance America would have been in dire straits. America only faced up to reality 2 years later, 1941, when the Germans other ally, Japan, attacked and sunk its Warships at Pearl Harbour.

For most young men National Service bred in them the discipline that would enrich the rest of their lives. Others were killed or wounded in far off places. Possibly the most tragic were those used as Guinea Pigs, to die prematurely from Cancer etc., due to the disregard for their health by those with power over them.

Four friends, Dave, Ernie, Robbie and Graeme are examples of the different views young males held at that time towards the subject of conscription and their experiences.

Although the other three tried to persuade him otherwise, big Dave was adamant, he wanted to be a soldier and he would sign on as a regular for three years, because of the extra money. His pals looked at each other in dismay; Dave was a slow moving youth with not an ounce of venom in his body.

The money bit they could understand, Dave hated putting his hand in his pocket and was always in the rear when it came to his turn to buy a round of drinks. After passing his medical he had no difficulty in achieving his objective. After an escorted visit to the camp barber and with his fair curly locks shorn, 'which didn't do his ears any favours,' he joined the rest of his Platoon of skull bared and ego deflated infantry comrades. Soon after being whipped into shape on parade and weapons training, he was posted abroad. His mission for the rest of his service was to try and capture elusive Greek terrorists on the island of Cyprus. At one point he was lucky to escape unharmed from a well-planned road ambush.

The Greek terrorist activities finally led to the Turkish invasion of the North of the island and partition. Dave finished his service physically unscathed, but with a less easy going side to his nature.

Unlike Dave, the last thing Ernie wanted to be in his life was a soldier. As he angrily told the others, "I'm no bloody hero and have no wish to be one, alive or dead."

With a steady girl friend, a well paid factory job, an active membership of the local Working Mens Club and the annual family caravan holiday, he was more than happy with his life. All he wanted to do was to get his National Service over as quickly as possible. After his basic training he got the posting he had dreaded the most, to the Malayan jungle.

An estimated forty thousand troops served in Malaya, supported by seventy thousand Malayan police and a quarter of a million Home Guard. All this manpower and expense to ferret out around eight thousand communist guerrillas, annoyed at being overlooked since the end of the Second World

War, who were causing havoc in towns, villages and rubber plantations.

After three months of jungle patrols, and fearing he would be shot by a mostly unseen enemy, Ernie was desperately trying to get a different posting. The humidity, blood sucking Leeches and a chance of catching Malaria, did nothing to help him adapt to army life.

Most of his Platoon suffered in varying degrees from sweat rash, due to the conditions they were living and working in. This gave Ernie the idea for a way out of his nightmare, a rather painful one it must be said. With a heroic sense of duty to himself, he rubbed his inner thighs and private parts with steel wool until they bled. The camp medics were baffled as to why Ernie's sweat rash was so bad and after weeks of treatment would not heal. Eventually they gave up and he was posted to the more healthy climate of post-war Germany to serve out the rest of his service, or as he put it, his sentence.

Robbie, a sturdy little youth was the youngest of the four. At the age of fourteen he was sports mad, playing scrum half in his school rugby team on a Saturday morning, and as a prolific scoring right winger in the village senior football team in the afternoon. Surprisingly considering his small stature most of his goals were scored with his head, from crosses and corners from the left wing. His goal scoring upset the team's burly centre forward, twenty-eight years old Howard Crane, so much so, he threatened to beat him up for not passing the ball more often. Joe Bent, an ex heavyweight boxer in the Royal Navy, and the teams centre half, came to Robbie's rescue with a huge fist in front of Howard's face, and a few quiet words in his ear, but Howard did have a grievance although his behaviour was way over the top. Like most strikers Robbie was greedy on the ball, but he never had the advantage of a day's coaching in his life.

On leaving school at fifteen, Robbie became a Painter and Decorator's apprentice. He picked this trade thinking it would be nice to work outdoors in the summer and warm inside in the winter. This was one of many errors of judgement he would make in his journey through life. Being an apprentice meant doing a man's work for six years with a much smaller pay packet. For the first two days he was taught the basics of the trade. How to mix and apply the various paints and emulsions, or distemper as it was then called, with colouring agents such as yellow ochre. Burning out the built up layers of paint in containers called kettles, which were used to appy the paint from, and being a general drudge to the boss Neville Fitch or Mr. Fitch as he liked to be called.

On his third day after a nerve jangling climb up three ladders, joined together in extension by ropes, he found himself standing on top of a large Dutch Barn with Mick Widdowson his elderly foreman, and their equipment. Mick tied a rope securely around both their waists, sat down, and then slowly lowered him down the curved side of the barn, holding a large tin of Bitumen and a paintbrush. It took him a week to paint the corrugated sides and top of the barn. Splashes of the tar-like Bitumen burnt into his skin as he dangled on the rope in the heat wave. It was just as well that he didn't know that the following winter he would be chopping ice out of Guttering, drying them out with a cloth, then painting the insides with spare leftovers of mucky paint. Working on the Stucco covered outside walls of a house in a snowstorm, wearing a Balaclava and an overcoat.

Neville Fitch would tackle any job at anytime. This included, standing on ladders eight hours a day, for weeks, burning off decades of cracked paintwork from the outside walls of Public Houses. The heavy, fuel filled BlowLamp held awkwardly as he stood up the ladder, and a Scraper that jolted his wrist, made it impossible to lift a drink to his lips at the end of the day. Soaking the grime and smoke covered interior walls of Pubs with Industrial Lime, mixed with water, dried and cracked his skin and stung like hell when it got in his eyes.

Sand-blasting the interior walls of ancient Churches, which created choking dust. There was one blessing; the Nanny State didn't exist so there was no need for safety helmets or equipment. You could still play 'conkers' without wearing protective glasses.

The Public House jobs also produced another serious health risk. Fitch would binge drink all day, driving them back home with glazed eyes and talking crap, with the battered yellow work van swaying all over the road. He also had a sadistic sense of humour. When Robbie was sixteen, Fitch took on another apprentice named Andy Dodson. On Andy's first job they were having a tea break in the workers hut, on a building site. Fitch sent the lad to buy a Sky Hook from a hardware store, this was the popular joke in the trade at the time, to play on new apprentices.

Fitch then put some yellow ochre pigment in a paint kettle and mixed it with the only liquid at hand, his own. As the embarrassed Andy returned Fitch placed the paint kettle on top of the partly open hut door. The kettle hit the youngster smack on top of the head as he entered the hut, knocking him out. Fitch had put his filthy mixture in a kettle with a heavy lead base. It was a month before the yellow pigment grew out of Andy's hair and scalp. He looked like a Punk Rocker long before their time. The Andy incident, poor wages and dirty dangerous jobs made Robbie's mind up, to get out of the trade for good. He knew that knowing the tricks of the trade would save him a lot expense in the future. After advice from ex-servicemen and looking for the best option, shortly after his seventeenth birthday he joined the Royal Air Force for the minimum period of three years. With no qualifications he was restricted to just two jobs. The one he got was to turn out more interesting than he could ever have imagined.

Before being accepted as a regular, he had a routine medical and was passed as A1, one hundred per cent fit. His first camp was at Cardington, in Bedfordshire, to be kitted out before going on to a square bashing camp for basic training. Cardington was also a training base for the Parachute Regiment. As he watched its recruits being drilled at double quick time on his first day at the camp, he wondered what the hell was in store for him. At nine p.m. it was lights out, he was bedded down in a Barracks with a bunch of strangers. It was New Years Eve he had never felt so lonely and miserable in his life as he lay awake and heard Church bells ringing in the New Year. It was snowing when they arrived at the R.A.F. base, West Kirby, on the outskirts of Liverpool.

As his group and others, from all over the United Kingdom stood to attention, naked as the day they were born, Robbie was surprised how well hung most of the little guys were compared to their six foot plus comrades. A medic Officer then went along the rows of recruits, lifting their penis with a baton-like stick to give it a close inspection.

One thing was for sure, the recruits felt so humiliated and embarrassed no one was going to get an erection. They then went to the other end of the large recreation hall, one at a time.

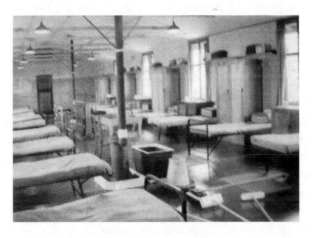

West Kirby, Liverpool.
Square bashing Camp Billet

Another medical Officer sat there in a comfortable armchair, with his legs crossed, smoking a pipe. At the Officer's order Robbie turned his back to him and bent over to touch his toes. Innocently unaware of Haemorrhoids and such, Robbie wondered what the man was looking for. Did recruits try to smuggle in pet mice or guinea pigs up there, or was he trying to see his Tonsils the hard way. After a thorough check up, it was discovered that he had a scar on his right eardrum and should not have been passed A1, as he was unfit for aircraft crew.

He was pretty sure the scar had been caused on a rain soaked, muddy football pitch when he was fourteen. The heavy, soggy football had hit him at close range, as he tried to avoid a mighty clearance from a hefty full back. The ball caught him smack on the side of the face and knocked him out. After five minutes he came round and finished the game. It was not until then, with his adrenaline back to normal, that he felt the pain and was told that blood was seeping out of his ear. It reminded him of his other fairly serious accident when a football had hit him on the hand, flicking it back and breaking a bone in his arm, just above his wrist. He was twelve at the time and sweating like mad from the shock, walked to a relation who lived nearby, holding his now misshapen right arm in his left hand.

After a four-hour wait at the hospital, and after being given gas anaesthetic, the bone was reset. The last things he saw before the gas began to work was a large clock on the wall and the Surgeon's masked face looking down on him. He dreamt that his head was on the end of the hour hand of the clock, and the Surgeon's masked face and one arm on the other, in his fist the Surgeon held a big meat cleaver. He woke up just as the man caught up with him. He then found the operating table was surrounded by a group of medical students, tears of laughter running down their cheeks. He went red in the face from embarrassment, wondering what he had been yelling in the terrifying chase while he was under the anaesthetic.

A few years later he had jumped out of his Dentist's chair in a daze after a tooth extraction and grabbed him by the throat. While under the anaesthetic he seemed to blame the last face he had seen for the pain he had not even felt. Something like a drunken lout with a chip on his shoulder.

How did our National game fall into the hands of a Foul Infested Football Anarchy? With the injury feigning, time wasting, shirt pulling, wrestling in the goal areas, blatant obstruction with arms and body to shield the ball. Goalkeepers now untouchables, treated like an endangered species and Referees running scared of, in their face, foul mouthed, pampered players. Let's hope the disciplined code of Rugby, its players and spectators, continue to set their exemplary conduct as an example for the youth of today to follow.

After the camp medical examinations and a black and white film show about Venereal Disease, which must have made some Airmen impotent for the rest of their lives, it was time to eat, but some just wanted to vomit. After a long lecture on how grateful they should be to the Crown and Government for giving them three free meals a day, they were marched to the cookhouse clutching their tea mugs and eating utensils in one hand behind their backs.

Later, in a state of confusion they were assigned to different Squadrons, either A, B, C, or D. Each Squadron had its own Drill Instructor, there was a strong rivalry between them to turn out the best intake. Each had his own room next to the large open plan Barracks hut. There was no escape from their constant nit picking. As they stood by their beds, being humiliated and shouted at, Robbie realised it must be harder for the older men who had finished their apprenticeships, some were married with kids. He was also glad he was small in stature, the bigger and older men were verbally abused more frequently. The Instructor knew that once he had them under his thumb, the rest would fall into line. In a nose-to-nose confrontation with one heavyweight, the saliva spraying mouth of the Instructor, voiced his contempt at full blast as he threatened to rip the man's arm off and batter him with the soggy end. The rest of them stood rigidly at attention.

Robbie was beginning to wonder if he had joined the best option. The worst insult screamed at him was, 'You funny little sample of worthless shit, why don't you do us all a favour and crawl under a rock and die'. This was for putting his webbing belt on upside down when half asleep, before a six o'clock in the morning inspection. After a week of spit and polish, D Squadron was beginning to look more like the finished article on the Parade Ground. They were told that towards the end of their training, an Inter-Squadron boxing tournament would be held. All boxing teams would be exempt from rifle drill to concentrate on Gym training. Although he had never boxed before Robbie joined the boxing team, to avoid the endless marching with his heavy rifle in the icy cold. Although he was not looking forward to the actual tournament, as there were some amateur boxing talent among the recruits, Robbie enjoyed training in the warm Gym, most of which consisted of thumping a punch bag, shadow boxing and some light-hearted sparring. You were also treated with some respect.

D Squadron.
RAF West Kirby 1953. Author is back row, far right.

The camp was practically shut off at this time by snowdrifts. The local Salvation Army women struggled through to serve them tea and biscuits from a caravan near the Rifle Butts. As they were the first women the recruits had seen for three weeks, they were a great morale booster. During the short training breaks the women's cheery banter and smiling faces, gained the Salvationists, and their Tambourines, a heart-felt respect from the grateful recruits. Even the comfort of a warming shower was impossible at this time, as the frozen water pipes had burst.

After six weeks the recruits were bursting with energy and their isolation in the camp, niggling them. Ugly arguments and fights were breaking out. This obviously didn't go unnoticed by the camp superiors. With a break in the weather it was announced they were to be taken for a night out, with a Ferry trip across the Mersey, to a Dance Hall in New Brighton. Robbie's eyes lit up at the news. At the age of sixteen he had started to get strong urges for closer contact with the female sex.

He became aware that the best way to do this was learning to dance. He joined a Ballroom Dancing School for beginners. At these sessions you formed two circles, with music playing in the background. The men stood still in the inner circle, facing out. The women walked slowly round in time with the music, in the outer circle. When the music stopped you had to dance with the female who had stopped opposite you. Because of his height this could prove embarrassing, as well as pleasing. On one occasion as he held close a young giant of a female, his eyes level with two mounds of white flesh, overflowing out of a half cupped bra in a low cut dress, she said in a very sarcastic manner,

"Are you a jockey then?"

Without taking his eyes off the thought provoking view in front of him he had replied, "No I am a stable lad, as you can see I'm used to handling muck."

One of his older sisters became engaged to an American airman, Frank Bowley, he and sisters, Ann, Elizabeth and Milly taught him to Jive. Rock and Roll he practised in a youth club in the nearby village of Glenfield. At the New Brighton dance, Robbie's rating went up the scale in the eyes of the Drill Instructors, who were on the alert for any trouble, and his mates. He was surrounded by females keen to learn to Jive and Boogie. He even managed to sneak outside for a quick smooch and fondle.

Three days before the Boxing Tournament the Sprogs, as they were called, were given an armful of Inoculations, for every disease they were likely to catch, if posted abroad. Robbie's arm swelled up to twice its size, from an infection. With a great feeling of relief and hidden glee he was told that any boxing or drill was not possible for a week or two. His Squadron won the most bouts at the Tournament, and there was a big celebration in the Airmen's Mess. Robbie tried to look disappointed as he was given consolation pats on the back for being unable to box. The FeatherWeight, who won, a fiery little Scouser knocked all his opponents out.

After their passing out parade they were given two days local leave in Liverpool as they waited for their postings. Robbie, with little money, booked in at the Salvation Army Hostel with a Squadron pal, Wayne Mooney from Manchester. Because of his unsmiling features and tight-lipped look, Mooney had been nicknamed Zippy. He had been a constant source of amusement on the camp and taken a barrage of verbal abuse, even being called a Mother F———. On one occasion he accidentally shot dead a seagull, sitting minding its own business on top of the twenty feet high wall, above the targets in the Rifle Butts. On their first day of freedom they went pretty wild with a party of locals. The Scousers certainly knew how to enjoy themselves. After some sightseeing, and a few beers on the second day they were just about skint.

In the evening they walked along Lime Street, passing two

heavily made up ladies standing on a corner, who looked at them curiously. In their uniforms and with short haircuts, they looked even younger than their seventeen years. With just enough money for two mugs of tea, they went into the nearest café. A little later the women who had been standing on the street came in and sat down beside them, asking where they were from and so on. The lads looked at each other uneasily when Marie and Sara insisted on buying them a meal. Sara laughed heartily as she saw the look that passed between them and said,

"Don't worry lads we're not after your bodies, we know what you get paid, we just want you to have a good time."

After watching them tuck into a big meal Marie and Sara gave them a fiver each before returning to their patch in search of some trade. The lads couldn't believe their luck, the women just wanted to mother them, and a fiver was around four weeks forces pay, part of which, you had stopped to be sent home to your parents. With beer a shilling a pint and a decent meal for around two shillings and sixpence, they both had full stomachs, hangovers and money to spare when they returned to West Kirby, the next afternoon. As well as the Salvation Army, Robbie now had a growing respect for women from the twilight zone.

The Squadrons postings were read out the next day. Robbie's luck was in, he got a home posting in Cambridgeshire to a base for Meteor Jet fighter planes, as a Barman / Waiter in the Officer's Mess. He had no idea what the job would be like but consoled himself by the thought that it had to be better than being on top of a Dutch Barn dangling on a rope.

A main road ran through his new camp with the airfield and guardroom on one side and the social and domestic buildings on the other. After being pointed in the right direction from the guardroom, with his kitbag on his shoulder he passed the bunker like clothing stores on his right. With the stately home appearance of the Officer's Mess and living quarters behind, near the back entrance of which, was a grim looking wooden building. It contained the reception and interrogation rooms of the C.I.D. the Criminal Investigation Department. On his left the all important Parade Ground, on each side of it were the Airmen's quarters in one storey brick buildings, containing four large dormitory's each, showers and toilets. At one end a medical centre at the other the N.A.A.F.I. - The Navy, Army, Air Force Institute. It took up one side of the square with a stage, bar and café downstairs. The upstairs was furnished with large settees and armchairs where you could relax. Behind the N.A.F.F.I. lay the Sergeant's Mess, Airmen's Mess and sports fields. Hidden from Robbie's view was a pleasant surprise, a four-dormitory building, which housed the W.R.A.F. - the Women's Royal Air Force.

He soon settled into his new environment after the harsh treatment endured in basic training, it was like being in a holiday camp. His job gave him an insight into life that money could not buy. During his service at the base he served food and drink to many a visiting dignitary including the Duke of Edinburgh, Marshall Tito of Yugoslavia and the Emperor of Ethiopia. A September Ball was held every year where the Officers, wives and lady friends were wined and dined in all their finery. During this event the staff were on duty for twenty-four hours non-stop. A weary Robbie on his way back to his billet and bed stopped at the N.A.A.F.I. for a quick drink.

He was awakened by one of the staff two hours later as she wanted to lock up. She was an attractive mature woman aged thirty-six. He apologised as he got up to go he hadn't known where the hell he was when he woke up. Although contracted to the forces the N.A.A.F.I. staff was more or less civilians and lived on the premises.

Rose who was new to the camp felt sorry for the fresh faced youth who looked out on his feet, and offered him the use of her bed for a couple of hours till she finished her shift. As soon as he hit her pillow Robbie was out like a light. He woke up four hours later cuddled in Rose's warm embrace. He learnt a lot from Rose over the next two years and her bedroom windowsill bore the scuffmarks of his many stealthy departures. There were also many great nights out down the local pubs with the girls and boys in blue.

The upstairs lounge in the N.A.A.F.I. was dimly lit and a popular smooching spot until some idiot took a bed up and left it with stained sheets and all. He became a regular player in the camp football team with time off work to train and quite a lot of travelling to other bases. A meal and free drinks were usually laid on in a Sergeant's Mess after a game, win or lose. One of his best mates was a jocular Cockney known only as Nosher. He had a very unusual job as the Warrant Officer's run about, and looking after the welfare of a number of pigs, on the outskirts of the base. What the hell the pigs were for, or whom they belonged to, nobody could find out.

One night he and Nosher were having a drink at the nearby village of Sawston. Two young Irish men and women started a conversation with them and insisted on buying rounds of drinks. Towards closing time the Irish group suggested they went for a skinny dip in the river at Cambridge. At this time R.A.F. bases were being attacked by the I.R.A. for rifles and ammunition. Robbie had just finished a week on guard duty, locked in a guardroom cell overnight with a field telephone, ready to phone the duty Officer in the Officer's Mess if there was an attack. It was a warm summer's night and with the suggestive talk of the two pretty young colleens adding spice to the idea, Nosher was all for a ride in the Irish groups car to Cambridge.

Robbie felt uneasy; their newfound friends were asking too many questions about the base. He voiced his concern to Nosher in the gents' toilet, so they made a hasty retreat out the back yard of the pub. He would wonder, for the rest of his life, if that night would have been a night to remember, for all the good reasons, or his instinct for self-preservation saved him from a nightmarish fate.

Another close friend was Pete Shaw, a cook in the Airmen's Mess. Robbie really enjoyed the soups, which were full of flavour, especially the chicken. Pete said to him one day,

"I've noticed that you love our soups, I'm on duty on my own tonight, if you would like to see the kitchens come round to the back entrance of the Mess tonight."

In one part of the kitchens were four very large vats connected to steam pipes, which were covered in an asbestos type material. Steam bugs were scurrying along the pipes and some had half drowned themselves in trays of tomatoes, laid out ready for breakfast on the spotlessly clean worktops. Pete raised the lid of a vat of chicken soup, with a large ladle he scooped up two chicken legs complete with feet, avoiding a few steam bugs as he did so. Now Robbie knew why the soup was so tasty, it contained one or two secret ingredients. He ate sparingly in the Mess from then on, eating in the N.A.A.F.I. and occasionally in the kitchen of the Officer's Mess. Pete told him that the Airmen's Mess was fumigated regularly but within a few days the steam bugs were back.

Halfway through his service Robbie got another lucky break, a three months posting to Celle in Germany during the summer. It was a training camp for Reservist Officers to keep them up to date with the latest fighter Jets. Each intake came for a fortnights training. Most of them were veterans from the Second World War and some had played a vital part in the Battle of Britain. As they were now civilians from all walks of life they mixed a little more freely with the other ranks.

Some invited Robbie on their trips to a night out in Hamburg, for a spot of window looking and nightclub entertainment. The camp also had an open air swimming pool, as he worked at night in the Officer's bar, he soaked up the sun during that hot summer as he lay by the pool. It was three months of sheer bliss. Shortly after he returned to Britain the front page story in the daily papers were about six airmen serving overseas who had come out of the closet as homosexuals. This was a criminal offence at the time and two of the ringleaders arrived at his home base under close arrest in the camp's C.I.D. headquarters. The Special Police were busy at the time with a serious case much nearer to home. A woman had an illegal abortion and two corporals from the medical centre disappeared after their room was searched. It was rumoured that a large glass jar containing a pickled object was discovered in a wall cupboard.

After two years of service his luck finally deserted him. He was sent on another attachment to the Bisley Shooting Tournament in Surrey. This was an annual event in which many V.I.Ps took part. For the lower rank military staff it was a tented camp in a soggy field, sleeping four to a tent with orange boxes to store your kit. Trousers were stretched on camp beds and slept on to try and keep them in shape. The toilets were trenches with buckets in and a plank of wood for a seat, all discreetly covered by makeshift wooden huts. The cookhouse was an open-sided tent and the shower blocks a cold running nightmare.

A month later he collected his train ticket from an unusually friendly and talkative Military Policeman, at the Bisley camp guardroom. He was surprised to be met by two M.Ps in a jeep who escorted him, under arrest from Duxford railway station back to the guardroom at his Duxford base.

The 'friendly' M.P. at Bisley had phoned ahead and reported him for being scruffy. As well as a lot of piss taking he was sentenced to seven days on Jankers. This involved visiting the guardroom twice a day for a full kit inspection and to be humiliated by a group of M.Ps.

They hoped he would lose his temper, so they could have their fun-time for a little bit longer. Shortly before the end of his service Lady Luck dealt a final winning card in the luck of the draw. He missed being sent to Christmas Island, in the Pacific Ocean, with many others. The object of the exercise was to witness the exploding of an experimental Atom Bomb. As the chosen watched the gigantic mushroom shaped cloud rising above them, a rush of contaminated air swept over them. Two mates and a cousin's husband, like many other unfortunates who were there, died prematurely from cancer.

British Governments to this day, in June 2011, still deny any responsibility and refuse compensation to victims and families. Perhaps we have become over the years, too accustomed to our men in suits neglecting our own, and trusted allies.

Thank God we still have a few voices like JOANNA LUMLEY.

The former Royal Air Force base at Duxford is now known globally as a British and American Air Forces museum, and a World Wars one and two Land Forces museum. Visitors include many relations and friends of those who served in the name of freedom.

Graeme was the eldest of the four. He had never been in steady employment and worked only for cash in hand. Most of his income came from buying and selling anything for a quick profit. He always seemed to have plenty of money to splash around and was generous to a fault. When he bought a top of the range Ford automobile there were suspicions that some of his wheeling and dealing was not above board. This guy was

RAF Duxford
Author is centre front

no fool and physically blessed in all departments. His fear of nobody and temper were respected in the area and anybody upset him at their peril. The death of his father from his war wounds, a few years after the Second World War, had left Graeme very bitter towards the establishment. Like all the armed forces his father had been promised a land fit for heroes on his return to civilian life. Unable to work he had spent the rest of his short life in poverty.

Graeme's mother found his National Service call up papers torn to shreds on her dining room table. He and his girlfriend, who was too young to marry in England fled to Scotland and were legally wed at Gretna Green. They then moved around Britain to avoid the Military Police. Six months later in Brighton, Graeme returned from fetching a morning paper to see two Military Policemen camped on his doorstep. He decided to leave the country, feeling no guilt about leaving his young bride without as much as a goodbye. When the novelty of moving from one place to another had worn off she had nagged at him constantly about being homesick and he should give himself up. He was left wondering why the hell he had married her in the first place?

He made his way to Felixstowe and boarded a ferry to Zeegbrugge. He spent the next four months travelling through Belgium, doing any work he could find and improving on the little of the French language he learnt in his schooldays. In some places life was made easier as the natives spoke mostly in English as well as their native Flemish. He eventually made his way to Paris and in a bar met Franz who was from Nuremberg in Germany. Like himself Franz was backpacking around the region and told him he was a plumber by trade. They decided to travel together for safety as much as for company. They had both been in some nasty situations on their travels, mostly in bar brawls after a few too many drinks, which had alerted the unwanted attention of the police. They travelled to Cannes and as their friendship strengthened after several brushes with locals and the law, Franz confided that he too was on the run. He was a burglar whose speciality was expensive antiques, which he sold through a corrupt antique dealer. The man had been caught red-handed with stolen goods and split on Franz.

It was not until they had made their way back to Paris that they realised they were being followed and watched. After seeing an advertisement for volunteers, the Legion Etrangere appeared to be their only escape route, they noted the contact telephone number. A recorded message in English gave them the address and directions to Fort De Nogent in the suburbs of Paris.

The fort was all enclosed and looked like a medieval castle, carved into the arch above the main wooden gateway were the words FORT DE NOGENT and below LEGION ETRANGERE. A small barred window opened in the gateway and they were asked to state their business. The gates opened, they were led across a large courtyard by a man in a sand-coloured uniform. At one end was a grass embankment with a stone archway with LEGIO PATRIA NOSTRA carved into the arch. They would learn later that this stood for 'The Legion is our Homeland.' They were taken into a large room with a desk and counter at the far end. Behind the desk was a thickset man, also in uniform, who told them in French and with gestures, to empty their pockets, rucksacks, and take off all their clothes. He then wrote down all the items and put them in sacks. They were given blue tracksuits plus running shorts and a pair of trainer-like shoes, all smelt old and looked second hand.

They were then taken into another building where an Officer sat behind a desk. He spoke to them in French and another soldier translating into English asked them why they wanted to join the Legion, to which they replied,

"For a military life and adventure." This they had been told was the standard answer by most people who wanted to join up.

They were then asked if they wanted a new identity, and for

the Legion not to tell anyone of their enlistment. They were then informed that they could not have a passport or driving licence or bank account, and were not allowed to get married for five years or contact anyone outside the Legion. If a Legion doctor passed them fit they would immediately sign five-year contracts. A quick medical examination followed, which they passed. They were then told that for the next two days they would undergo a series of tests, physical and mental plus a security check, if they failed any of these they would be back on Civvy Street. If selected, they would go to Castelnaudary for basic training and serve in the French Foreign Legion for five years. It had taken them just four hours to sign on for the minimum five years. After the harsh reality of basic training they both settled into the Legion way of life. They were the types of men who needed the adrenaline of danger in their lives.

They fought together in French territory for four years and were involved in many skirmishes but they also enjoyed the social side of life in the Legion with well run brothels, bars and a comradeship second to none. It was during their last year of service that they fought what was to be their Waterloo.

The North Vietnamese near Ha Tinh ambushed their platoon, as the French Foreign Legion fought the communists before America became involved in the Vietnamese war. Franz took the brunt of a grenade blast and lost his right leg and left foot. Graeme escaped with less serious shrapnel wounds, they were both stretchered to safety by their comrades. Franz survived to marry, and father two daughters and settle in France. After two months in hospital Graeme was fit enough to finish his service. Unlike their neighbours across the English Channel the French looked after their Foreign Legion who fought and died in their name, and awarded them with French citizenship on completion of their service.

With this in mind Graeme felt safe now to return to England. As he was uncertain of the reception he would get back home, he booked into a hotel near the social club where his mother had played Bingo once a week, before he had fled. It was as if time had stood still, she sat at the same table with her eyes down, marker in hand, busily crossing off the numbers as they were called out on the string of game cards on the table. At the end of the game she looked up and saw him as he stood by the bar. Her face was expressionless, as he walked over to her. The first words she uttered to him were,

"You are divorced and she sold your car."

When family and friends, who presumed he was dead or rotting in some jail, heard his story, like the prodigal son he was welcomed back into their lives. After the excitement and danger of life in the Legion he found it hard to settle in his home surroundings and decided to make a fresh start to his life. During their time in the Legion, Franz had passed all his knowledge of antiques on to him, so he decided to put all that information to good use. He moved to Brighton for closer access to London and the Continent and became involved in the antique business, dealing in Britain and mainland Europe.

This enabled him to see Franz and his family on a regular basis. He became a very wealthy man with an extremely hectic social life, mixing with the rich and famous, but he never forgot the debt he owed Franz for making it all possible. When Franz, unable to endure his immobility any longer, committed suicide when his youngest daughter was sixteen, Graeme set up a trust fund for his friend's family to make sure they were well provided for. He had decided long ago that the ups and downs of married life were not for him and was quite content with a mistress on each side of the English Channel, each unaware of the others existence.

On his seventy-first birthday, a week after his annual medical check up, when he was told he was in prime condition for a man of his age, he died in a place he loved, under strange circumstances. He was in one of his favourite antique shops in France when a large First World War poster caught his attention. He collapsed without any warning onto the floor. Staring down at him and pointing an accusing finger was the face of General Kitchener. In bold letters the poster stated, 'YOUR COUNTRY NEEDS YOU.'

A WORRIED FAN

Whatever happened to the days
When footballers and fans were pals
Played the game for peanuts
With a seat for friend in Stand.
They didn't lead the jet set life
Or live on Caviar
Just fish and chips
On match day nights
Or a pint with fans in bar.
Some may have had five bellies
But they kept a low profile
Boots that protected ankles
With solid toe for power,
A ball of heavy leather
When wet it weighed a ton
Could turn the head to jelly
If not timed right on a run.
Fans not segregated, often shared a flask
Kids were handed over heads
Down front for view of park.
Come back Stanley Mathews,
Busby, Ramsey, Shanks.
And all who played the game
Wore their club shirts with pride.

RUGBY IN UNION (INTERNATIONALS)

National pride in afternoon
The stadiums fill with anthem's tune
Proud England stand, red rose on white
As 'God Save the Queen' the crowd sing out,
Kiwis with nostrils all aflare
Chant the 'haka,'leap in air
'Land of My Fathers' from massed Welsh choir
Emotions for country does inspire.
In shirts of gold Aussies composed
Feel victory is their abode.
A cheer erupts from Irish and French
Fast running game supporters' sense.
Before the start of Murrayfield show
'Flower of Scotland,' chills the foe.
Flags and Mascots join Shamrocks, Leeks
From all nations who union teach.
Argentina and Italy
Now with us mix.

LOVE ROMANTICA

There is a well-known saying, 'It is better to have loved and lost than to have never loved at all.' Most songs are also linked to romantic love, such as, 'Love is a many splendoured thing.'

This may be so, but it can also be a recipe for disaster as millions of divorcees, battered wives and husbands, and the anguish suffered by families as a whole, can testify to. It is also responsible for countless suicides.

Romantic love is a potent chemistry between two people that can devour common sense, decency and free speech.

It is a sad fact that most people have to reach the wisdom of old age, to experience the merits of solitude, contemplation and contentment with ones lot, if good health permits.

DIVORCE

It breaks the bond
Of all involved
As papers served
On marriage cold.
All branches of
The family tree
Axed with a finality
No longer stable
On emotion road
When shedding of
The family code.

MONDAY MORNING

You may well know the feeling
As you sit on edge of bed
Stomach aches from Sunday lunch
Late drinks swim in thick head.
You stagger to the bathroom
Teeth are not in glass
Some pranksters stuck them grinning
In the soap bar by the bath.
Groomed and dressed minus one sock
You make it down to hall
A jobby waits by doggy's side
Lost sock lies by its ball.
The car won't start; train's running late
For bus the rush hour queue
Impatiently awaiting
The boss with Monday blues.
You get your cards, yes it's the sack
Whatever will you do?
The car is due its M.O.T.
Arrears in mortgage new.
Back on the street you slide into
A pavement takeaway
You think your ankle's broken
In curried chips with tray.
Twenty pounds they bill you
For ambulance and crew
To sit six hours in casualty
Wondering, why you.

No welcome home from offsprings
Wife or family pets
All eyes and ears are riveted
On the television set
Yes you're right you've guessed it
It's Coronation Street repeat
Curly's trying to fathom
A barmaid who's petite
She simpers hot air in his ear
But suffers from cold feet.
You crawl upstairs in great distress
Slide between the sheets
Monday's almost over
It swept you off your feet.

KIDS

You cannot tell what you have got
From angel face to ugly mop.
Will innocence stay or recede
As in mean streets their footsteps lead.
Will they get into booze and smokes
Or on the drugs minds grow remote.
Will they go bent, rampage and steal
Or stay as hoped on honest trail.
It all is in the hands of fate
Parenthood for all cannot be great.

GANGING UP ON DAD
1980

Icily calm he waited on the dark landing as her stiletto heels clip clopped on the paving slabs, to the front door. The car she had come home in had been backed onto the tarmac car space below his bedroom window, with the interior light on, windows down and the car radio at full blast. The male pick up, she had been snogging with, drove off as she unlocked the front door. The respectable neighbourhood had certainly seen and heard plenty to gossip about over the past two years. With all his anger spent, after being humiliated over a long period of time, he calculated his chances of getting away with what he planned to do. It was half past two in the morning, and his two daughters were asleep in their back bedroom. It would only take him a second to slip back into his room, as she hurtled backwards down the stairs, onto the marble tiles below.

His mind flashed back over the last seventeen years of married bliss and hell, as she opened the door.

They met at a Rock and Roll dance. She was a slim, blue eyed beauty with long, naturally wavy black hair and a pleasant personality. An amateur soccer player of some ability he had played the field, in more ways than one in his twenty-seven years. He was no angel or virgin, that was for sure, but with most of his friends now married, he felt ready to settle down. His thinking at that time was, there must be more to life than just having a good time. If only he had realised how well off he was.

Six months into their courtship, Irene, or Blossom as her dad called her, left her job on the production line at a biscuit factory to work in a large High Street department store on a smaller wage packet. About this time' one of Blossom's girl friends told him that although Blossom was great company on girlie nights out, she did like to flirt and be the centre of attention. He had shrugged these comments off as being unimportant.

One Saturday afternoon after playing soccer, he had a quick bath and decided to meet Blossom out of work. He had invited her for the first time, to tea at his home and to introduce her to his parents. With his car in a garage for repair, he went by bus into the city. As he walked up to the High Street Blossom was walking towards him, hand in hand with the young manager of the shop. As they appeared to be in some deep discussion, they did not see him and he darted into a shop until they went by. He followed them to the bus station where they had a mouth to mouth kiss and a loving embrace, before parting company. Still unaware of his presence, he followed her onto the bus and sat behind her. She turned around with a startled look in her eyes and her mouth agape in shock, as he whispered in her ear,
"Got yourself a new bloody boyfriend have you?"

Groby Championship Team
Author, far left, front row

She quickly regained her composure. "It's not what you think, a man has been following me, and Clive is good enough to walk me to the bus station every night."

He did not believe her and finished the affair. Six weeks later they met accidentally, a tearful Blossom again protested she was innocent of any wrongdoing and they began seeing each other again. He was genuinely more than just fond of her, but Christ! How many warnings did he need? After they had a passionate romp one sunny day in a hayfield, he was about to come face to face with reality.

Three months later he asked Blossom's parents for their permission to marry her. He was surprised when they refused, saying at the age of eighteen she was too young, but they would be happy for them to get engaged. He told them that was all right with him, but she was three months pregnant. Her mother would have been better prepared for the unexpected news if she had been sitting down. She staggered back a few steps in dismay. She was a buxom lady and he thought for a moment she might keel over. He could not understand their attitude; after all, they had been courting for over a year.

Blossom was without doubt the out and out favourite of their four children. Her mother was in many ways a likeable woman who worshipped her husband George. He, on the other hand, was a self-centred extrovert, who kept her and the family short of material comforts, while boasting of his Bank balance. The stairs and bedrooms had no carpets or covering, just plain untreated floorboards. The whole house was in need of a major overhaul. Sloppy birthday and anniversary cards with great bunches of flowers and the annual fortnight at Butlins Holiday Camp, seemed to make up for all of George's shortcomings. The family had been going to Butlins for many years, with George usually winning a trophy as, 'King of the Camp,' for his comical antics, which, up to a point, could be rather amusing. His affection for Blossom was probably enhanced by her singing ability and personality, which also won her many Butlins awards.

Feeling a bit guilty about getting Blossom pregnant, he painted the outside of his future in-laws house, while Jolly George and family enjoyed their annual fortnight in the limelight, at Butlins. The wedding was to take place the week after they arrived back home.

Blossom insisted on a white wedding, with all the trimmings although four months into childbirth, also, a honeymoon in the Scottish Highlands. This worried him, he explained to her that after paying for the wedding reception and holiday they would be broke, even his car was ready for the scrap yard. Blossom told him in all innocence not to worry, she had nine pounds in the Bank. Not a princely sum even in the early nineteen sixties. Her five pounds a week, after bus fares, from her job at a City Bakery had been dutifully handed over to her mother every week. One thing he admired about Blossom was the fact that she respected her parents in every way.

The wedding took place on a pleasant summer day. Blossom looked a picture in a flowing white wedding dress, which disguised the not yet prominent swelling around her midriff. Everybody appeared to enjoy themselves at the reception, with violin and accordion playing guests from Scotland providing some lively entertainment.

The only sour note came, as they were about to leave on their honeymoon. His brand new mother-in-law in front of the other guests, thrust her head in the car and shouted at him,

"Look after her or you will be bloody sorry."

After a glorious week in the Scottish Cairngorms they headed back to reality. He had rented a room off a middle-aged widow, in a Coronation type setting, two rows of terraced houses with a corner shop, and the Abbey pub at one end and the Great Central Railway line at the other, just a half a mile from the City centre. There was no bathroom but the rent included the use of the small kitchen, gas boiler and outside loo.

He could sense the tension between Hilda the landlady, and his young bride, from day one, but beggars can't be choosers. The street was just twenty yards from the sock factory where he worked two shifts, from 6 a.m. till 3 p.m. and 3 p.m. till midnight, plus six hours every other Saturday morning. A maternally minded next door neighbour made sure he didn't sleep in for work, by banging on the bedroom wall at 5 a.m. until he banged back. Blossom had already packed her job in. Hilda fussed over him like a broody hen, much to Blossom's annoyance, telling him to visit the outside loo at least once a day, as she was convinced her husband's death from cancer was due to chronic constipation.

"Keep your bowels open," she would repeat. He nodded in agreement while thinking to himself, 'That cold, damp outside loo is enough to make anyone stiffen up.'

He was surprised how quickly he settled into his new lifestyle, which also had its fun times. One of the iron struts holding the wire spring bedstead, snapped underneath Blossom and himself, after a severe jolting, rolling them in a tangled heap onto the floor. They looked at each other in shock before bursting into fits of uncontrollable laughter. Hilda was far from happy.

The Abbey pub held a table skittles competition when Blossom was eight months pregnant. She and another baby bellied lookalike reached the final of the ladies singles.

This produced a string of dry witted but inoffensive comments. They celebrated her win with a free pub meal, baked spuds, black pudding and mushy peas. Later, Blossom's rendering of the song, 'Scarlet Ribbons' brought a hush to the inebriated gathering, setting up free drinks for the rest of the evening, even Hilda got legless.

Two weeks later on a Sunday afternoon, Hilda went out for the day. Blossom, although the baby was not yet due, thought she was going into labour. Mavis the street's Hairdresser, who had five kids, advised Blossom to sit in a bath of warm water. She would know for certain if she had a show. As they didn't have a bath Mavis, who lived in Cardinal Street lent them a large metal one. He could imagine the curiosity and titters of amusement behind the lace curtains as he staggered the street length into Wolsey Street, with the bath above his head. Blossom had lit the gas boiler and with considerable effort he pushed the bath into the narrow kitchen. After filling the bath and sitting in it for two minutes Blossom told him in a calm voice to fetch her ready packed suitcase from upstairs. Although in a panic he drove her safely to the City Maternity Hospital in Bond Street. Their baby daughter was born an hour later. When he got back to Wolsey Street some time later, Hilda had returned. Unaware of what had happened and unable to move the bath, she was bailing it out with a saucepan and cursing them like mad.

The baby was healthy but only three pounds in weight. Mum and baby were kept in hospital for another three weeks. As Blossom was breast-feeding he was advised to take in a supply of Guinness to build her up. He made sure she had more than plenty and enjoyed seeing the faces of the new dads as he sat with a glass of the black stuff at visiting time. Meanwhile he had got a mortgage on a house, four miles from the city. Two days before his family came out of hospital he partly furnished it and moved in. Blossom knew nothing about their new home her gratitude was overwhelming.

While all this was going on George wanted to buy a car and asked him if he would help by giving him driving lessons. This he did for many months until George passed his driving test. He never asked for, or was offered, any recompense for his assistance, but while visiting garages to find his father-in-law a suitable vehicle, he was told,

"If you are ever in a spot of bother, money wise, don't you be too proud to ask me for a loan."

Two years later his second daughter Tara was born, with no complications. His battered old Morris 1000 was off the road, in need of a new engine. Remembering his father-in-law's words and thinking it would give George a chance to repay for all he had done on his behalf, he asked for a loan and was told there would be no problem. When the car was ready he phoned George telling him the car would be ready for collecting from the garage the next day. Knackered after all that been going on and having just finished his early shift, he waited for George to phone, or arrive with the cash, but all in vain. In the end, bleary eyed; he caught a bus to the in-law's house. He again told George that the car was ready to collect. The old windbag just puffed his pipe and kept mum. Two hours later it dawned on him what George was up to. He was waiting on him asking outright for the paltry forty-five pounds or even beg for it.

Without a word he got up and left, absolutely furious. What made matters worse was the reaction to the news by his wife, she did not say a thing, Daddy could do no wrong. A quick call to a sister and he had the money within the hour. He wished to hell he had never given Jolly George the option, any of his own relations would have given him their last penny. George turned up flashing a wad of notes weeks later and told where to stick them. Relations were strained from then on.

Starting married life with no capital and a baby on the way had not been easy, now with two children and a wife to support, a steady income was necessary. On the plus side he now had an incentive to work. On an overnight stay at his dad's, a coalminer, a near tragedy occurred.

He was shaving in the upstairs bathroom when he heard a strange gurgling noise. He turned his head and was horrified to see Jill his three-year-old eldest child, drowning in the bath. She had crawled upstairs after him and fallen into his father's soaking pit clothes, which dragged her under. Luckily he got her out before any real damage was done. It made him realise how vulnerable kids can be. This incident made him slightly over-protective for the rest of his two daughters' upbringing. Apart from that the early years were pretty uneventful. He taught them to ride their bikes, swim, ice and roller skate at the Granby Halls. A homemade sledge used in Bradgate Park was great fun. His one regret was his wife not joining in on these activities, preferring visits to relations or knitting and crochet work, which helped a little with the family budget. She was also very reluctant to get out of bed before ten in the morning.

To her credit she was a tidy housekeeper, and doting mum when she surfaced. Their arguments were few and far between and sexually their relationship was as good as ever, until Jill, the eldest girl reached her teens. The girls were well behaved and doing well at school, Tara, the youngest, in particular. When he was on early shift he took them to the school Disco and drove them home for there own safety. He found out later how much they resented this and other restrictions, because mum was letting them come and go as they pleased, when he was on afternoon till midnight shift.

Money was still a problem as they were now running two cars, on top of all other expenses, off his wages. He did not mind as Blossom, so he thought, was staying at home for the girl's wellbeing. His wife took a seven till nine evening typing course at the local college.

As the course progressed her homecoming became later, until she arrived home one morning at 2 a.m. He waited up getting more agitated as the time went by. Her flushed excited face reminded him of that fateful romp in the hayfield, her thin cotton dress rucked high. They had a blazing row, he asked her what the hell was going on?

She said that a group of the women on the course went to each other's houses afterwards, for a drink and chat, that was all.

"Why the hell didn't you ring and let me know, you selfish bitch? I've been sitting here worrying about you, and in four hours time I'll be flogging my guts out in that smelly, sweaty sock factory."

"I didn't think you would wait up," she replied, without as much as a 'sorry.'

He told her from the start that if she ever met someone else he wanted to be the first to know not the last. A week earlier the husband of her best friend told him over a drink he was stopping his wife attending the course, but just shrugged his shoulders when asked why? It was if the man was trying to tell him something. Blossom's flirty nature was always in the back of his mind, like a festering sore.

A month later he received a telephone call at work. Blossom's car had broken down in a village, on the other side of town, near a Police Station. It was ten o'clock at night she was on her own. The car chassis had broken and it went straight to the scrap yard. A week later she said, "I want another car."

"If you save up the deposit I'll pay the rest on credit," he offered.

"I want one now," she screamed.

"If that's the case you better get out of bed in the morning and start working to pay for one," he shouted, his temper now at boiling point.

Shortly afterwards she started work in a city shop, afternoons only of course. She had chosen it carefully, not for the money, but the attention and flattery her ego craved.

He began to feel isolated from his daughters as well, working shifts didn't help, and he saw little of them. What he did not know was the girls had been introduced to mum's lover months ago, taken out and treated. In their eyes Blossom could do no wrong.

As the matrimonial bed was now like an icebox, he decided to sleep downstairs. She refused to admit there was anyone else. He even asked her if she had turned lesbian.

Two nights after sleeping downstairs she amazed him by pleading with him to return to their bed, as she missed him. He refused her generous offer.

He wondered at the time why his daughter Tara never

81

asked why he was sleeping in the front room, when she kissed him on the cheek and said, "Bye dad" before going to school, on his late shift.

A week later he answered the phone one morning, a male voice asked to speak to Blossom. Before he could reply she scampered downstairs in a blind panic, snatching the phone from his grasp. It was then that he knew for certain she was having an affair, Blossom as a rule never rushed out of bed for anything. Grabbing her by the throat he demanded to know the truth. Her lover was a married man who had already left his wife and four children, in anticipation of moving in with his bit on the side. He could hardly believe it, with the mortgage nearly paid, the girls grown up, they were heading for the best years of their lives. It was also difficult to accept that after seventeen years together she did not really know him, as she said tearfully,

"I still care for you, and when you move out and David moves in, I want to visit to make sure you are all right."

He stared at her in silence for a while trying to make some sense out of what she had just said.

"What makes you think I would be stupid enough to want visits from a woman who is callous enough to break up two marriages involving six kids, for her own selfish pleasure? If, and when I move out I don't want to see, or hear from you again."

His first move was to visit a Solicitor to see about a divorce. As he was not involved with anyone himself, he was told to let his wife go to the expense and trouble of getting one. As he was determined to stay in the family home, which the Solicitor strongly advised against, he must resist being violent, no matter what the provocation, or he would be evicted.

His second trip was to Sergeant David Glover's place of work, which curiously was near the spot where Blossom's car had broken down, to confront him.

Luckily, considering the state of mind he was in at the time,

Glover was off duty, or so he was told. A senior Officer interviewed him in a cell for some reason. After hearing all the details the Officer stated,

"Well, we are only human you know."

As they were talking about a desk Sergeant with twenty years service and not some rookie cadet, he felt his blood pressure rising,

"For Christ sake, just tell your human buddy to keep away from my wife and house until this bloody mess in sorted out. I want this interview put on report, so don't try any cover up."

He had gone to the Police Station wearing an imitation leather jacket in need of repair. He thought, 'to hell with it, I'll treat myself for a change, to some new clothes.'

He shook his head in disbelief when Blossom saw him and said, "Oh, you're looking nice."

He spent the weekend at his parents two bedroom flat. When he returned home on Monday morning she called him up to the bedroom and said angrily, "That was a dirty trick you played on David."

He was beginning to wonder if she had any feeling of guilt at all, she was talking like a single woman with no family responsibility. She and Glover had been taking him and Glover's wife for a couple of mugs for at least the last two years.

Brother-in-law Michael who had been through a similar trauma in his first marriage, gave him a right earful when he heard of his situation.

"Bloody hell, you have been too good to them, she is still sleeping in your bed, your girls won't talk to you but enjoy the home comforts your hard work has given them, and are even backing their mother! They are old enough to know better. Have next Monday off work, I'll come over, when she and the girls are out, to help make some changes."

True to his word he came equipped for house rearrangement. The main bedroom was cleared of Blossom's belongings, which were dumped in the tiny spare room.

The twenty-six inch television set went upstairs into the main bedroom and was replaced by a tiny black and white set. A hole drilled in the main bedroom door was then fitted with a Yale lock, hey presto, he had his own flat. Later that day he visited his in-laws. He had a good relationship with his mother-in-law, obviously they knew what was going on. He told them straight that no way was he going to walk away from all he had worked for, without a fight, the mother shed a tear. George smoked rapidly on his pipe, but kept his thoughts to himself.

When he returned home he got a bit of a shock, the adulterers were sitting in Glover's car awaiting his return. His first reaction was to pick up a large boulder from his front garden with the intention of throwing it through the car window, which was parked on the road. A few feet from the vehicle he thought of the Solicitor's warning and why they were taking this risky action. She must have phoned him and told him about the lock on the bedroom door, so they now knew he meant staying in the house. As an Officer of the law, he would be aware that the only way to get him out, would be a charge of being violent. Dropping the boulder, he walked to the front door, turned round and leaning against the wall with arms folded stared them out, he was hoping that Glover would be tempted onto his property. After five minutes Blossom got out of the car, and unable to look him in the face walked past him into the house. As Glover drove off he thought with a smile, 'got you David that is the biggest mistake you have made yet, and I'm going to make you pay for it.'

Next day a registered letter was sent to the area Chief Constable, stating,

'Dear Sir, my great admiration for our British Police Force has been shattered, by a married Police Sergeant sitting outside my home in his car with my wife, trying to provoke me into violence. His Police Station was informed before this incident of his affair with my wife, told to put the matter on report and advise him to stay away from my wife and property.'

A plain clothes Police Officer in an unmarked car, visited the house by appointment the following week, interviewing Blossom on her own and then him.

"Your wife has admitted all your allegations against the Officer concerned are true, do you wish to make an official complaint?"

"Yes," he replied.

"I strongly advise you not to do so, it can cause all sorts of problems. We do not condone this type of behaviour by an Officer, let us handle it, he will be reprimanded, the facts will go on his file, which will deny him the chance of future promotion."

The veiled threat in the Officer's first few words made him feel pretty sure if he did not agree to this Officer's suggestion, he might finish up with some harassment, or a blemished file himself. He had reason to feel worried. He knew from the Landlord of his local pub, The Stamford Arms, that some plain clothes Officers who usually only used the lounge bar, had been making inquiries about him in the public bar where he went for a pint or two of beer, once a week. Being in the local sports paper many times over the last twenty years for his goal scoring ability, they had an innocent motive to talk about him

Football and cricket trophies with long service tankard.
Robert Fallon Jr.

and gain information on his lifestyle. They must have been very disappointed with their feedback.

After a few minutes thinking it over he reluctantly agreed to let them handle it. He was then handed a document to sign, which included a paragraph stating he had no objection to the offending Officer attending domestic call-outs. He refused to sign the document. When asked why, he replied in a calm voice,

"If the accused Officer ever visits a home of mine again, now or in the future, I will do as much damage as I possibly can to his physical health, with whatever means possible."

For some reason the Officer went white around his gills and quickly erased the offending paragraph.

A fortnight later he arrived home from work to find a hysterical and tearful Blossom was waiting to greet him. She had received a Dear John letter from her lover telling her he missed his kids and was going back to his family. It was no wonder she was so distressed. This was the man she had boasted loved her so much he would do anything for her, and would never let her down. It became known later that he was summoned to face his superiors, and given the choice of finishing the affair or being dismissed from the Force. The chastened Officer's love for Blossom was no match against losing his job. Just before his retirement from the Police Force he was promoted, these late promotions seemed to be a regular occurrence. Was there, as rumoured, a bigger pension involved?

Blossom pleaded with him to have her back using the girls as a lever.

"The girls need you and I need you," she wailed.

It was too late to wipe the slate clean, he could never trust her again or the betrayal by his daughters. Although not a cuddly, hands on sort of dad, he had tried to do his best for them. Some people tried to convince him that it was not the girl's fault that they had been influenced by their mother and were too young to understand. This theory he dismissed after his first visit to a launderette after Blossom's panic flight to the phone and her confession.

The launderette was empty apart from a young woman and her five-year-old daughter. As the young woman explained to him, at his request, the working of the washing machines, the little girl tugged at her mother's skirt. The mother looked down at her daughter and asked,

"What is the matter?"

The child looked up with a worried frown and said, "I am telling my dad."

Even from this innocent encounter with a strange man the child felt her family security threatened. From this experience he realised his daughters had little or no respect for him, and didn't give a toss whether he went or not, as long as they were well provided for.

He now understood why the girl's never asked why he was sleeping downstairs, and the youngest girl had come in one morning, kissed him on the cheek and said, "Goodbye dad."

The reason for this became clear shortly after he knew the truth. Mummy displayed for him to see three small vases each containing a single rose, and Valentine cards from Sergeant Glover. Maybe he should have taken lessons from Jolly George and the romantic David on how to beguile the ladies.

For a while things settled down, the family used the downstairs while he used the flat, eating out, and stopping at his parents on weekends. By doing this and working his shifts, he avoided them. He paid more maintenance than he needed to for Tara and all the household bills. Jill the eldest daughter, had left school but didn't have a job, but she did have a twenty-three year old layabout boyfriend who came to the house, with her mother's consent. The former longhaired, studious fourteen-year-old was now a Skinhead with all the clobber. It was now obvious that this had not happened overnight. The girls, like their mother had been leading a double life, the one they didn't like for his benefit. It was at this stage he made a fatal mistake, instead of moving out he stayed. All his capital was tied up in the house and he was back to square one, saving up for a deposit on another house. Blossom was not going to get the satisfaction of him moving in with his parents or renting a property.

Then he received a six-page letter from a social worker telling him to move into his parent's spare room, as he was upsetting his daughters by staying in the house. Who was this faceless idiot who had never seen or spoken to him, but was telling him what to do without any authority, to remove him from his own home? Arriving home from work a few nights later an empty bottle of Aspirins lay outside Blossom's bedroom, with the door half open, he ignored it. The next night he found a note slipped under his door asking him to give her another chance, and he would not regret it.

The next day he told her he would not have her back even if she were the last woman on earth. It was a pity he did not take heed of the old saying, 'Hell has no fury like a woman scorned.'

The next week on his early shift they really started ganging up on him. Every night as soon as he went to bed Jill would put her record player on full blast, in the front room below. Blossom was night clubbing, a few weeks later she was cooking curries every day and children's Indian clothing was washed and hung over the hall radiators to dry. He was told she was having an affair with her Solicitor's clerk, an Indian gentleman whose wife had left him with two children. Her Solicitor, so he was informed, took a dim view of this and somehow put a stop to the relationship.

He picked up a letter on the stairs about Skinheads written by Tara. Amongst its contents was the fact that her best friend had seventeen piercings in one ear and her dad didn't mind. A sixteen year saving policy for Jill matured he didn't get as much as a thank you. The money was spent on taking her boyfriend on a holiday abroad some weeks later. The constant noise at night from the record player was taking its toll and playing havoc with his nerves.

One night he got out of bed went downstairs and trying to keep his cool, asked Jill to put the volume down or use her earphone set. Without saying a word she lowered the volume. He dropped into bed with a sigh of relief. Five minutes later it was increased to full blast. Rushing downstairs he shouted,

"Switch that bloody thing off or I will put my foot through it."

Her reply stunned him, "Who do you think you are, you F——g C—t, you do and I will have you sorted out."

He had never even heard her swear before let alone threaten him with violence. In a fury he shouted,

"You will do what?" Then flipped her across the top of her head with the palm of his hand.

"Mum, he's hitting me," she yelled.

In came Blossom who after trying unsuccessfully to kick him in the privates, calmly picked up the phone to call the Police. He had been well and truly set up.

A Policeman and woman arrived, took statements off the two complainants before having a private word with him. They were very sympathetic towards him, which made him wonder if a certain Police Sergeant's involvement in this drama had been mentioned, out of spite.

"I can't believe what I have just heard," said the young lady Officer. "Your wife wants us to charge you with Grievous Bodily Harm on your daughter, and evict you from the house. As you are obviously not violent we refused, but if I were you I would be very careful, they mean to get you evicted one way or another."

There was one consolation, Glover must have been through a torrid time as gossip spread through the Area Constabulary.

A fortnight later he was issued with a private summons for Assault and Battery against Jill, his daughter.

He informed his Solicitor, who was not very happy about him losing his cool, after managing to stay in the family home and put up with the situation for over a year. He asked if there was anything he himself could do to save his daughter going through the ordeal of the court proceedings. The Solicitor replied,

"Are you serious, don't you realise they are not just trying to get you evicted, but you are now facing a prison sentence as well. I want to know the exact words your daughter used to provoke you?"

The Juvenile Court waiting room was packed when he arrived at ten o'clock. A court official shouted for everyone's attention, then asked them all to leave and return at 2 p.m. apart from himself, Blossom and Jill. This really got him worried as he had imagined it would only take about half an hour at the most. It was three and a half hours before the three Magistrates reached a decision. When questioned, Blossom lied saying his daughter's face was all red where he had hit her.

Jill, who came into the court room later was given a demonstration by his Solicitor on the different amounts of pain and harm that can be inflicted with a raised arm, a fist and the palm of the hand. She eventually admitted she was only flipped across the top of the head, thus proving her mother was lying. As well as this, the Magistrates would have the report about what condition she was in physically, from the two Police Officers who were called to the house by her mother. She also could not remember the last time her father had hit her but settled for five or six years earlier. She was then asked not to be shy or embarrassed and tell the court what she had called her dad. No way was she going to say F——g C—t, so she said, a Bastard.

Blossom had also put in a claim for substantial maintenance payments for herself. She was awarded the princely sum of five pence a week. The Magistrate decided he was not a violent person and need not leave the family home. But if he as much as raised his arm in a threatening manner again he would face serious charges. When he left the Juvenile Court he was a very relieved man. At the nearest newsagents he bought a paper and asked for five brand new pennies in change.

He confronted his wife and eldest daughter. "Here is your first maintenance payment," and placed the pennies one at a time in front of a downcast Blossom. His daughter did not appear to have got over the shock of her court ordeal, and he felt she was for the first time realising the enormity of what was taking place, she avoided eye contact. Before the Court Summons he had received an anonymous letter telling him that his wife was in a relationship with an Arab student half her age.

His mind jolted back to the present when she was half way up the stairs. The cold blooded horror of what he was about to do hit him. With a shudder he stepped back into his moonlit bedroom, silently closing the door. He sat on the edge of the bed in a cold sweat, his head in a spin, staring at the sturdy coat hook on the bedroom door, twisting the chord of his dressing gown in his hands.

IT WAS OVER – TIME TO FLY THE NEST.

THE AFTERMATH

Strange as it may seem, and unthinkable at the time, the 'Ganging up on Daddy' episode had beneficial and positive outcomes for all concerned.

According to gossip and other information it became known that the Police Sergeant's wife kept a close eye on her husband's working and social activities from then on giving him little opportunity, if he desired, to be unfaithful again.

The harsh lessons from their parent's marriage and divorce must have resulted in a change for the better for the two daughters, they finished up with trouble free lives and successful careers in catering and advertising.

Blossom married her nineteen-stone Arab student, who was half her age, which gained him British citizenship. He turned out to be a devoted husband serving her every whim. When she died, a decade and a half later, he spent a week mourning at her graveside. He then collected the hundred thousand pounds he had her insured for, sold the family home and left the district. Blossom had died suddenly from a brain tumour. Some people questioned whether her irrational behaviour during her first marriage was linked to this tragic ending to her life. A close member of her family said she also hated, more than most, the thought of growing old.

There are details in the following story titled, 'The Nearly Man,' of a chance remark to his Solicitor during the Juvenile Court drama, that set Blossom's first husband on a literary journey he had never even thought or dreamt of. The pleasure he got from the variety in his imagination was priceless, not to mention the social benefits from Craft Fairs, Poets Conventions,

Book Signings and many other activities where he learned the skills of numerous trades.

An invitation to write a poem on the Royal Wedding for a book titled, 'A Royal Romance,' publishing date July 2011, gave him much satisfaction, after all he is well versed in the marriage stakes.

A copy of the book is being sent to the Royal couple by the publishing company, to commemorate their wedding.

In his later years he began a friendship with a lady, who asked for nothing more than his company now and then. With a strong maternal instinct she insists on looking after his welfare with a range of toiletries, medicines and delicacies in gift bags. Life is certainly worth living.

THE WEDDING OF THE YEAR
2011

To H.R.H. Prince William
And Kate Middleton his bride
Whose wedding day coincides
With my seventy fifth birthday
In the year 2011 on April 29th.

————

You have with wisdom waited
Until mature in age and thought
Before final commitment
To share lives in wedlock.
For some close relations
Emotions will run high
As memories come flooding back,
Others hardened from experiences
Will hardly blink an eye.

————

May your lives be a joyful duet
With harmony your theme
As you take the world stage
And start to live your dreams.
I hope the Press will be kind
to you as they gather
And newspapers are not full
Of opinionated chatter.

————

In remembrance of the lady
The nation held in high esteem
I felt compelled to write
The words came from within.

————

A FLOWER OF COMPASSION

So much to give, taken too soon
A flower plucked from us
In full bloom.
The disabled, sick and dying
You comforted with a smile
Compassion was your forte
With elegance and style.
We laid a wreath
With tears of grief
It stretched the world wide
For you were special – one apart
Princess Diana – Queen of Hearts.

———

I hope you both will embrace
The humanitarian cause
And with dignity, humility
Set an example for us all.

———

With sincere regards.

THE NEARLY MAN

Ann Summers sat perched on a chair in her glittery black dress with her perfect curls falling delicately on to her shoulders. Sitting in a corner of the hotel's large banqueting hall she gracefully sipped her wine while watching the behaviour of those around her. Why had she really bothered to come anyway? A whole bunch of pretentious strangers slapping each other on the back and congratulating each other. It had seemed such an excellent idea to try something new, but now it felt incredibly wrong. Whatever had possessed her to attend a poet's convention?

She had arrived in Washington D. C. the previous day, as the personal assistant to a millionaire boss who owned, with other assets, a large toy and craft shop in the Midlands of England. The manager of the hotel had given her a complimentary ticket to the convention while Steve her boss, and his mistress, attended an international trade fair on the other side of the city. With all the celebrities she was informed would be present, plus a free Buffet it had seemed too good an opportunity to miss. The much-respected ex-President of America, Bill Clinton, was to honour the proceedings with an opening speech and awards distribution.

Her only knowledge of poetry was limited to the over rhymed ramblings of an ex-boyfriend, or to be nearer the truth, an ex-old man friend, who also dabbled in writing children's books and adult short stories as a hobby. They met in her previous employment as a secretary in a hosiery factory. Short in stature an average looking guy and a divorcee, who was old enough to be her father, he definitely was not the man of her dreams.

Author at Poets Convention, Washington DC

He worked as a well paid mechanic–knitter on alternate shifts, among the factory sock machines. The noisy, oily, hot and fluff breathing conditions were uncomfortable to work in, to put it mildly. His work attire consisted of an assortment of T-shirts and grubby jeans. The gossip around the factory of his many escapades and his unusual hobby had aroused her curiosity in a man she would have usually not given a second glance.

It was also said that he had vowed not to get sexually involved with female workmates, though his keen eye for long shapely legs had not gone unnoticed. A well-known lager drinker, his occasional binges were common knowledge, the fact that he never seemed to lose control of his senses amazed most people. A house warming for his new abode, after his divorce, was talked about for many years. With the house overflowing with guests, invited and uninvited, he had been left with cigarette stubbed carpets, shelves of empty miniature whisky bottles,

97

mountains of beer cans and a scattering of skimpy clothing.

They first got friendly at a factory dance. She was surprised to see him looking quite presentable, in up-to-date clothes, with an after-shower glow about him. At the time she was taking lessons for her gold medal in ballroom dancing. He asked her for a dance, although his technique was a bit suggestive, he could move his feet from modern to rock and roll without treading all over her. They started dating, managing to keep their meetings secret from factory gossip for over a year. Sexually, they were more than compatible, much to her delight. She had a high sex drive and he was more than willing to satisfy her desires. With his vivid imagination there was no chance of their intimacy becoming stale. She was reasonably happy.

Adultery by his wife after many years of marriage had made him very wary of commitment. After his divorce he had found that he was still a faithful, one woman at a time, man.

Before meeting her he had enjoyed two, four-year relationships. He had made up his mind after his marriage break up, to keep his life as hassle free as possible, by not getting involved with married women and not to have a full time house-sharing relationship again. He was quite happy looking after himself. At least he had been honest with her and she was pretty sure that she could change his mind to her way of thinking.

His first affair was with a very religious spinster named Angela, who up till then was a forty-year old virgin. She cooked him delicious Italian and Spanish meals, fortified with red wine, in a candle lit setting.

On overnight stays at her home she would insist on towelling him dry after his shower, while his full English breakfast was frying on the stove. She was, without doubt, a lovely lady in every way for any male who wanted pampering to death. After four enjoyable years Angela was introduced to a man who fell head over heels in love with her, he proposed and promised to buy her a luxury bungalow. Angela then gave Robbie the choice, either marry her or they were finished. They parted on friendly terms and as far as he knew, Angela was still living happily ever after in a bungalow made for two.

Monica was a complete contrast to Angela. He had to be very careful what he said, as she took everything she did not like to be personal. The crunch came, in their relationship, when she asked to see a board game he had invented about marriage and divorce. He had jokingly remarked to his divorce Solicitor,

"I think I will make a board game about this, you could not make it up."

His Solicitor encouraged him with the idea and recommended a printer who was also going through a divorce. The making of the game proved to be therapeutic and probably saved his sanity. Although the game was partly humorous, Monica's reaction to the game cards stunned him and put him off trying to market it.

"That's not me and that's not me, I would not do that to anybody. I'm not like that at all."

The more cards she scanned the more agitated she became. He became so alarmed he took the game from her. She stormed out of the house, screaming at him, "You will finish up a lonely old man." He never saw her again.

As she sat alone with her thoughts in the now crowded banqueting hall, Ann Summers wondered why on earth she had stuck with the eccentric guy for almost nine years, even if it was difficult to find a man who wanted a ready made family.

At the tender age of seventeen she was pregnant, a shotgun wedding to her boyfriend from school days followed. By the age of nineteen she was the proud mother of a second son. With husband Darrel in steady employment at a potato crisp factory and a promising scenic artist, the future was looking bright. They had been allocated a council house on the outskirts of the city, with an open green belt area at the front. She had been happy and content, but it was not to last. Darrel became restless and started acting like he was single.

Late nights out with his 'mates' became more frequent, then gossip reached her that he was having an affair with a pretty, young shop assistant. She confronted him,

"I didn't know you have a 'mate' called Alison."

Although startled, he just shrugged his shoulders and refused to talk about it. Feeling utterly humiliated she put up with the situation for the sake of the children, deciding to bide her time.

When her sons were old enough to fend for themselves she took a part time job. This gave her the independence she needed. With the rent book in her name she had her cheating husband evicted and started divorce proceedings. As a lone parent she had not been short of admirers, including a married Spaniard who became over-possessive, even though he refused to leave his wife.

A strapping toy boy who left her in the lurch after she taught him about the more intimate enjoyments of life. The adorable, romantic Richard who would be waiting on pay day outside her place of work, with a large bunch of flowers, then 'borrow' money off her and forget to pay it back. During their relationship she found out he had secretly married someone else. Why did she have the misfortune to pick the wrong men? She was beginning to wonder if all men were alike. The thing she liked about Robbie was the freedom he gave her to live her own life. After four years she persuaded him to buy her a ring, just for friendships sake. It was not the three thousand pounds ring she had casually pointed out, but she settled for one at his three hundred and fifty pounds limit.

He was furious when he received a card from her parents congratulating him on his engagement to their daughter. She should have known then that he would never commit himself fully. To be fair, he had helped towards her financial security by talking her into making investments for her future, and buying her rented council house. As a long-term tenant the huge discount on the actual buying price made her a very happy mummy. He also took her and the lads on their first holiday abroad, to the Spanish island of Majorca, paying for nearly everything. He had however, become rather annoyed for some reason as she treated herself to a one hundred and fifty pound leather jacket towards the end of the holiday.

Holiday's abroad on their own had followed. On a cruise in the Mediterranean a tape of his poetry given to the ship's Captain resulted in an invitation to the ship's bridge as it docked at the island of Ibiza. He also taught her to drive a car and gave her an interest-free loan, to be paid back when she pleased, to buy one. Their nine-year relationship ended when her boys left home in their mid-teens. She had taken it for granted that he would marry her when this happened. Somehow she managed to talk him into a shopping trip in the city, trapping him in a shop full of wedding dresses. He watched, with a sullen look on his face, as she inspected them. Ignoring his mood she decided to up the pressure on him, by suggesting they sold both their houses, bought a large bungalow and move in together. The property of her dreams was up for sale a short distance from her present home. There was a slight snag, it would cost as much as their two houses combined.

His reply shattered all her expectations. "Why don't you sell your house, which is worth a lot more than mine and move in with me? If it doesn't work out with us living together you will have enough money to buy a house like mine, no mortgage and a nice nest egg left over."

It had taken a minute to recover from her dismay before replying, "You haven't even got a proper garden."

She had now reached the limit of her patience and stormed out of the shop as he stared glumly at the most pretty white wedding dress with its flowing train. For two months he made no effort to contact her, so she wrote him a rather nasty letter, spilling out her pent-up anger. He had used her kids for years as an excuse for not taking their relationship any further. When they finally left home he then used his poetry, children's books and other literary work to hide behind. It was time he came out of his cocoon, opened his eyes and faced reality, instead of living in a fantasy world. She was bored to death with his lifestyle in general and being treated like an escort girl, apart from not being paid two or three hundred pounds a night. Did he not realise how much she wanted him that his attitude was making her ill and depressed? It was time he got off his backside and spent more time trying to please her for a change. Was he just another wimp with big ideas but with no bottle to carry them through? He ignored the letter so she went to see him, and told him any feeling she had for him was gone.

"Good," he replied. "That will make it a lot easier for you."

She left without a backward glance, seething with mixed emotions.

Her thoughts were cut short by a hand resting lightly on her shoulder. A man in a white tuxedo stood by her side. "Excuse me, are you on your own?" he asked.

"Yes, I am," she replied, feeling slightly flustered.

"May I buy you a drink, and join you?"

She could not believe her luck. He was of average height, with neatly groomed fair hair, a strong jaw line and a smile to die for. John Hughes was a Canadian publisher and entrepreneur and attending the convention as a guest. By the time they sat down to dine before the speeches and presentations she felt completely at ease in John's company. She had fallen in love with him at first sight and he was a bachelor with no ties.

To a round of applause Bill Clinton stepped up to the podium and gave a lengthy speech on the values of literacy and the importance of morality in family life. The drinks flowed as they were then entertained by top recording stars. By the time the awards ceremony took place everybody was in a state of happy intoxication. During the interval she found out that John's feelings for her were mutual and he proposed that they spent the rest of their lives together. She had never felt as happy in her life, her dreams were about to become reality.

The buzz of conversation around the hall ceased as the award ceremony started with medals of merit being awarded to many people for their contribution to literacy over many years. But her attention was on John as he whispered seductively in her ear. Suddenly she felt him stiffen with eyes riveted on the podium and stage. She followed his gaze and nearly fainted from shock. Looking ill at ease and rather dishevelled, Robbie was on the stage to receive an award for his contribution, over many years, to literacy. He had aged considerably since she last saw him, and all her bitterness towards him was forgotten at that moment. She even felt pleased for him that he had at last got some reward for his dedication. She was well aware of the work that went into his hobby.

To her surprise John sent a waiter to invite Robbie, with award, to join them at their table. She quickly told him, without any details, that he was an old friend from many years ago. When John told her he thought that Robbie could be of some value to his business, she could not suppress a smile, as a naughty thought passed through her mind. The self-centred, sheltered existence that Robbie treasured might just collapse around him in a wave of publicity.

FACTORY HARASSMENT

She is a wages clerk
Dress style is demure
To cut down on harassment
As she walks the factory floor.
Daily runs the gauntlet
Of whistler, groper, pinch
And arm over shoulder
Touching awkward bits.
Now don't get me wrong
Our Jan is no prude
Will sit on knee
Smudge your lips
In Christmas party mood.
But our Clive has her puzzled
He uses different ploy
No way would he
Touch her thigh
Or other ways annoy.
He is the answer
To many a maiden's prayer
A bachelor with brand new car
And a boat on Windermere.
He also keeps the budgies
Jan has had invite
To coo with him
Stroke little breasts
In aviary one night.
He calls her his little virgin
I think he's overkeen

She soon will be a grandma
But Clive he has a dream.
To see his favourite henbird
Rocking as she steers
While he puts away the anchor
On a lake called Windermere.

THE NEARLY MAN –
IN QUESTION

Would born with a silver spoon
Have broadened my horizons
Or ambition fed brought on stress
To start a chain reaction?
Might I have been a statesman
Believing in my spin
Or courting sleaze and vice
To bridge the gap between?
If I had reached the pinnacle
As a novel writer
Would I have slipped, lost my grip
As critics pulled me under?
Creativity by connection
Put in the spotlight
Millionaire or weakest link
No doubt would find me out.
As a sporting personality
My nature leans to Jack the Lad
Not training with desire.
If the ladies in my life
Belonged to upper crust
Would they be put off?
A nearly man in limbo
Paranoid of great divide.

TIME WAITS FOR NO MAN

Candyfloss clouds were the only interruption in the blue sky, beneath them the hustle and bustle of everyday life and sun-tanned tourists shop window gazing carried on as usual. Children were splashing and laughing in the hotel swimming pool while on the beach promenade, the elderly sat on benches and let the slight breeze blow them down memory lane.

He stood on the balcony of his hotel room, four storeys up in the Spanish holiday resort of Lloret-De-Mar and surveyed the scene below with mixed feelings. It was his first holiday abroad for 24 years and his first holiday on his own since his divorce. The feeling of isolation at East Midlands airport after a decade and a half of family holidays in Britain with wife and children by his side, now left him feeling hesitant and uneasy. The speed and steep ascent of the jet's take-off had taken him by surprise, thrusting him in a state of shock against the back of his seat.

His first flight to Lloret had been in a propeller-powered aircraft, with the rivets popping as it built up speed on the runway for a slow gradual climb into the clouds. The memories of that journey and holiday in the late 1950s came flooding back. A bus trip from the Midlands to a small airport south of London. The noisy drone of the plane's engines as it made its way to an isolated airstrip on the French border with Spain followed by a terrifying ride in an ancient bus, over the mountains into Lloret. What is now around a three hour journey had taken, including a minor bus breakdown, 24 hours. Hotel staff were lined up along the seafront awaiting their arrival, to carry the luggage to the handful of small hotels that existed then, down narrow, winding side streets. The holiday cost him 38 Guineas for a fortnight, equivalent to four weeks wages, with free bottles of local wine at mealtimes. There was no air conditioning in the hotel or en-suite rooms, hotel swimming pools with shower were not available to the budget holidaymaker, or anyone else in Lloret at that time.

He had travelled with two pals, Drew and Pete. Drew was a born romantic with an easygoing nature and Pete a no-frills guy with a dry sense of humour. They also palled up with two London lads, Max and Terry, on the long trip out.

They were all on the same hotel wing as two English girls, Joan and Sheila. Drew was soon working on his chat up lines to Joan, trying his hardest to impress, he had a genuine crush on her. It all went horribly wrong for him a couple of days later when he trotted to the communal toilet in high spirits. It was situated at the end of the short corridor, in full view of Pete as he rested on his bed with the room door open to let in some much-needed fresh air. Unfortunately the love struck Drew had not locked the toilet door and found himself staring dumb struck and open mouthed, at a blushing Joan, with his shorts around his ankles. Joan fled back to her shared room with Sheila in a state of shock. When Drew finally made an embarrassed appearance he found Pete rolling around hysterically on their bedroom floor.

After a gutsy apology to the new love of his life later that day, their holiday romance was on again. They became inseparable and it became obvious to the others that this was no passing fancy. Towards the end of the first week as a party of them walked along the sea front one moonlit evening, Drew took Joan by the hand and walked her across the golden sand to the water's edge. As the others watched he swept Joan into his arms in dramatic fashion as a freak wave swept up the beach engulfing them both. Drew, in a light grey suit and suede shoes took it all in his stride, trying to console a spluttering Joan who, with bedraggled hair, looked down on what had been her best evening dress, in disbelief. Drew's misfortunes made the dry-humoured Pete's holiday a great success.

Joan's companion, Sheila, must have been warned by her parents about the trouble virile young men can bestow on the female species. It was difficult to get her face to break into a smile, let alone anything else. He himself had tried his luck with a thirty-five years old divorcee who had joined their group.

Sadly, she was not interested in being bedded by a toy boy, one named Robbie in particular. They all met regularly at a six-lane wooden skittles alley, where young Spanish lads replaced the skittles for them and rolled the wood balls back along wood troughs for a few Pesetas. There was also a small bar and dancing area. It was one of the few places of entertainment, and stood like an oasis among acre upon acre of olive trees, which were draped with fairy lights around the entrance to the bar. The owners had a daughter in her early teens that helped to serve food and drinks. Max, the Londoner, was fascinated by the pretty young maiden and spent his entire holiday in romantic expectation sitting at the bar. They tried to tell him he was wasting his time, as it was difficult then to even walk along the sea front with a Spanish girl unless her mother or granny tagged along as chaperone. But Max would not listen to anybody, he had eyes and ears for nobody except the adorable Miranda.

As he stood now on the balcony a quarter of a century later surrounded by towering hotels and entertainment centres, he could not believe he was in the same place, it had completely changed with not an olive tree in sight. It was as if the once sleepy little resort had been wiped off the map. He was at The Flamingo Hotel in the centre of Lloret; his bedroom with another balcony was at the back of the hotel facing the rows of balconies of another hotel twenty feet across the narrow side street. Sleep was impossible from midnight until dawn. 'Oh Flower of Scotland' to 'Land of my Fathers' with more than a few tearful Irish laments thrown in, bellowed out as the whole

109

street joined in like a massive choir. Exhibitionists had a great time flaunting their bodies, most of them were not a pretty sight.

The Sangria was flowing freely all night long with the hotel corridors reacting like echo chambers every time a room door was slammed shut, the noise then vibrated through every room on the floor. Top of the bill in this never-ending entertainment was a character named Princess Sheba, a formidable looking woman weighing twenty stone plus, she was dark skinned and dressed in colourful flowing robes.

Sheba was married to a skinny little redheaded Welshman named Barry with their six snotty nosed kids in tow, aged five to thirteen. The kids ran wild all through the hotel and were addicted to the cigarettes. Sheba and the slightly built Barry saw life through a permanent alcoholic haze. They enjoyed telling all and sundry that Sheba belonged to the Royal Family of Tonga. She would make a dramatic entrance on to her third floor balcony, with her screaming backing group, around the midnight hour. For hours on end she would rant and rave about the English swine, lager louts and whores. Angry and witty comments about Tonga cannibals, Welsh sheep lovers and who had fathered her brood, would rebound on her like a torrent. It was all very entertaining, a street theatre from a wide species of life, most of whom were full of youthful energy.

On the second night of his holiday, as he was about to venture out for the night, he had stood at the entrance to his hotel looking across the brightly-lit main street. He could hardly believe his eyes, almost opposite, hidden between two towering hotels with flashing neon signs was the tiny entrance to the old skittle alley, lit up by a few flickering fairy lights. With mixed emotions he made his way towards it, wondering if the young daughter had managed to keep it. He could still visualize her in his mind and to be honest had actually had the hots for her himself, mind you, who in his right mind wouldn't have? To his surprise the parents were still there, serving drinks from behind the little bar at the side of the unchanged skittle alley. Apart from a few added laughter lines, they were exactly as he remembered them.

"Excuse me," he asked them, "Do you have a daughter named Miranda in her late thirties or early forties?"

"Yes," replied her father, with a slight frown. "Why do you ask?"

He explained that he had been in Lloret 24 years ago and often came to the bar. Maybe they would remember a young Englishman named Max who was on holiday at the same time, and spent all his time at the skittle alley chatting to their daughter.

"Well, we should remember," said the father with a twinkle in his eyes. "Max came back as often as he could and eventually they got married and set up home in London. Our nineteen years old grandson is coming over next week on holiday. We are having a big party and we would love you to come."

The party lasted all day and well into the night. Dan was the image of his dad, Max. He told the lad of his dad's so-called wasted holiday spent chasing his mother. Dan laughed as he said, "Wait till I get home, I won't half pull his leg!"

It was an enjoyable and unforgettable experience, party and all. It had also become clear that the perseverance of Max on and after, his holiday had transformed his life as a member of a multi millionaire's family. His father-in-law Miguel had owned all the acres of olive groves that were now the holiday centre of Lloret –de- Mar. After selling his land to property developers, apart from the skittle alley, he then invested a large part of the proceeds in buying land around the Spanish coast, before the tourist boom took hold and airports opened up for direct flights to Spanish holiday resorts. He smiled at the thought that now and again Max must chuckle to himself when he remembered the friends of many years ago who were angry about him wasting his holiday.

Miguel also told him that he and his wife Marie kept the

skittle alley open more as a hobby than a business, although surprisingly it still made a profit. With no money worries they were more than content living as they had since they wed. Their priorities could not be faulted. He spent many happy nights eating and drinking with the family and their friends.

During the second week of his holiday he managed to doze off one humid afternoon with the patio doors, leading on to his bedroom balcony, wide open to let in some much needed air. He was awakened by the sound of a heated argument from the apartment of the Welsh – Tongan 'rarebits' in the hotel opposite.

As he looked from his balcony to see or hear what all the commotion was about, the large figure of Princess Sheba staggered on to her balcony with the slight figure of enraged husband Barry on her back with one arm wrapped tightly around his beloved Sheba's throat. From a combination of booze, his loud mouthed wife and six 'out of control' kids, Barry had finally snapped. He hung on grimly as the screaming choked in Sheba's throat and she collapsed in a crumpled heap. Rob gave a sigh of relief, tonight he might get some sleep. In fact, things turned out a lot better, Sheba was speechless for the rest of his holiday with a badly bruised throat.

On conclusion of this basically true story it may be of interest to some readers that Drew and Joan from his first visit to Lloret kept in touch, got married and are still living happily ever after, with a few embarrassing moments thrown in, somewhere in England's Midlands.

THE DIAMOND COMPANY
1994

FRED   There is something strange going on across the road Doris.

DORIS For goodness sake Fred, stop being nosy and get me a cup of tea.

FRED   A gang of men have barricaded themselves in on the pavement and dug all the slabs up.

DORIS So what! Who is it this time, gas, water or electric?

FRED   You might as well get up and see for yourself, its pension day, time to spend, spend and spend.

DORIS Ha! Ha! Ha! Very funny, I'm not budging till I've had my cup of tea.

FRED   There's a young yob dragging a fully grown Rotweiller along the gutter, I think it's reluctant to meet its next victim.

DORIS Maybe he's training it to be a guide dog.

FRED   One of the gang has started up a little machine and it's scooping a trench down the middle of the pavement.

DORIS Well you never know they might be scooping a doggie trench and if they are still there tomorrow they might come across your remains, if you don't put the damned kettle on. who the hell are they?

FRED   Well it's not the usual lot, or the Council, but there is a big sign saying they're digging for diamonds.

DORIS   Come off it Fred, don't make me laugh. There is as much chance of finding diamonds under those slabs as us getting a decent pension.

FRED   No need to be sarcastic I'm just telling you what it says.

DORIS   Sarcastic, who's sarcastic? Just imagine all the doggie trots under slab level. What does it say on those scoop bins? Clean up after your dog. Crap a slab more like.

FRED   Come on Doris, you know you are a dog lover at heart.

DORIS   I am! I am! I have always gone out of my way for under dogs and I don't believe that they should be trodden on.

FRED   I bet there is nothing you would like to see more than them all pampered to death.

DORIS   You're right there, now stop nattering and get me a cuppa.

FRED   Edwina Curry has just come out of Major's at No 10, what with the barricades and all, she doesn't know if she is coming or going.

DORIS   Well it gets harder to make up your mind as you get older, but credit where it's due she has been a good neighbour to John over the years, they are always in and out of each others. She also helps feed those fat cats of his, I don't know where he finds the money to keep them all.

FRED   Oh no, not him again.

DORIS Not who again?

FRED   That young trouble maker Tony Blair's just turned up.
He is giving poor old John a right ear bashing. Hang on
a minute, I don't believe it, I think he is actually trying
to help John find a way out of No 10.

DORIS Trying to get him buried more like. Ten years hard
labour would wipe that permanent grin off his face.

FRED   That Gillian Shepherd's just come out from behind her
net curtains. She is giving the workmen a right tongue
lashing. Just as well she lost her walking stick when
some kids mugged her last week.

DORIS Fred, that's not funny, that could have been me.

FRED   Well kids will be kids probably it's just the modern
way of playing tag. It's a hard life for kids nowadays
what with all the temptations they face and rich food
that we never had. It's even driving the ruddy cows
mad.

DORIS Got an answer for everything haven't you Fred, you
will be telling me next that it's a good job we have
plenty of do gooders, to molly coddle the little
blighters.

FRED   Ken's just come out of No 11, showing some interest, he
is looking a bit flushed, bet he has been on the booze
filling that big belly again before the prices go up in
tomorrow's budget. Isn't he supposed to be on a
budget diet?

DORIS I believe he is, according to Tessa May who just opened that new shoe shop.

FRED He looks a bit top heavy to me. It's hard to believe he once ran a national health club. I think I will have a word with him and try to find out what the heck's going on.

DORIS For goodness sake shut the window, you're letting all the hot air out and you're not going anywhere until I get my morning cup of tea in bed, then you can set about the tripe and onions ready for lunch.

FRED Here you are Doris, sorry there's no milk, the milkman's late, bet he's digging for diamonds. I'll be back in a jiffy.

DORIS Anymore cracks like that and you'll be digging in the airing cupboard for sheets and blankets for the spare bed.

FRED I'm back Doris, are you up yet?

DORIS No I'm not. Have you found out yet what is happening?

FRED Well I've heard some tall stories in my time but this lot takes the biscuit. The workers said straight-faced that they are really digging for underground television, best I've heard since Rupert Murdock sent his son to buy him a sky line. Ken got excited again and began to stammer a load of nonsense.

DORIS Cheeky devils. What's all this about a sky line?

FRED Well, Rupert sent his son to the corner shop for a sky line. His son asked him what it was for. Murdock told him 'tongue in cheek' it was for capturing sky. His son fell for it hook, line and sinker.

DORIS   Well we all know with Rupert that the sky's the limit.

FRED   There is something fishy going on. I can't put my finger on it but there is not a bum cleavage in sight and not one of those men are leaning on a shovel. I'm going to the Police Station, it might be open by now.

DORIS   Alright but mind what you are stepping into and bring back some milk, I'll have another cuppa before I get up.

THE MILLENNIUM BUG

Coughing and sneezing it appeared in our midst as fireworks, costing millions at taxpayers expense, were lit and the Thames on fire was promised we Wonderland Brits. Bug's body was made of a green ball of slime with protruding black eyes above a glowing red snout and antenna that quivered as it begged, 'Help me out.' It had been around the world spread its germs then interfered with our systems until we shivered and threw up, with evil intent Bug struck at the pounds until they withered away ounce by ounce. It then weakened disabled each inch, foot and yard until with the threat of being locked up, strange foreign measurements took over our land. Brits fishermen it reeled in on a tight quota line, with foreign detachment it netted them all, to make them housebound on sick pay or the dole. In desperation some turned to crime but they were soon tagged or sent to jail with a fine.

A continental named Euro with marriage in mind came to Wonderland Britain in search of a bride, he bumped into Bug who gave him the flu, now he's weak at the knees with his plans all askew. A Mr. Sleaze and wife Mandy tried in vain to miss Bug by hiding in Harrods, disguised as two mugs. In France Bug had listened to what every working Brit knew, the continental advice sent his snout glowing red hot, 'Make your way across the channel by whatever way you can for their lies the land of Wonderland Brits who would surrender their all to make him real fit with housing, social benefits and welfare state aid, Parliament, the Queen or gallery called Tate, Brits would even give Spice girls to make him feel great.'

Bug made it to London where streets were gold paved laden with cheap booze and thousands of cigarettes taken from the lorry he hid in at Calais, he sold them to Brits without the 'over the top' tax. Printed on the packaging it stated quite plainly, 'Made in London' for export only by land, air or sea. Social Services contacted Bug to give shelter and food, advised it on form filling to make its life good.

Feeling real settled as it spread coughs and sneezes with Wonderland Brits it felt quite at ease. Bug then made its way to a tent called The Dome, his antenna had zoomed in on it as he started to roam. He queued up for hours as people were told the body inside was a sight to behold. Alas, Bug was told at the front of the queue, there is no entry for a Bug such as you. To the National Health Service he was given a note, a full body change for free could be sought. The Brits searched high and low for an intensive care bed where Bug could lay its bug ridden head, nowhere in Wonderland was there one to be found, only refrigerated lorries with stiff bodies inside.

With taxpayer's money taken from young and old, back to France the Do Gooders transported this thing. Although delayed there by lorry and farmers blockades in a ward next empty corridors Bug finally stayed, while top surgeons spent months on Bug's body remake. The generous Brits wished him good health, Bug thought what a soft touch, they are really swell. There is no doubt about it Bug will be back to the Wonderland Brits with their Santa-sized hearts. Bug came as a warning to one and all, look after your roots or head for a fall.

FIORD SPLENDOUR

As a special treat on his retirement, he booked a luxury cruise on a ship called the Saga Rose. The holiday got off to a great start, as they waited to board the ship they were entertained by a jazz band and sat down to enjoy the refreshments provided. The ship's crew were lined up on board in their smart uniforms to greet them and show them to their cabins. The ship had everything you could wish for, as well as a swimming pool, casino, grand ballroom, library and gym. There was a daily newspaper of activities and trips ashore. Nothing was too much trouble for the staff, even to folding the covers back on your bed and leaving a mint, and petals on the pillow.

The food would have been the envy of many a television chef and laid out on the plates so artistically you felt guilty disturbing it. He sat at dinner with some of the most interesting

"Saga Rose", Norway.

people he had ever met. One, an 84 year old ex-army Officer, who was fitter than most men half his age, spent an hour each day in the ship's gym. He was great company with many stories to tell.

The Jewish lady who spent nearly four years of her childhood in a concentration camp called Belsen. Now in her 70s, she ran a successful business, supplying interpreters to Government departments, helping translate for many immigrants who could not speak English. Another lady worked in her youth as a model in a famous Fashion House. Being the same size and shape of the then Queen of Sweden, the dresses ordered by the Queen were tried on her first to make sure they fitted perfectly. After her marriage, she and her husband bought two Rolls Royce motor cars and spent many years driving very important people around London and the Home Counties for a living.

Then there was James from a middle class family. At the start of the Second World War he happened to be on holiday in France while his parents were in England. Unable to return home, he was held by the German armed forces in occupied France, until the end of the war.

Although it was no picnic he was fairly well treated, and returned home in reasonably good health. Another lady, a retired barrister, would have them in tears of laughter about the comical side of law and order.

The final dinner companion was a bubbly, five times married American lady, who was now a widow, but intent on enjoying her life to the full. They teamed up together for many of the trips ashore. On one trip a small boat, called a Tender, took them ashore from the ship, which was anchored in a fiord with towering snow covered mountains all around. They boarded a coach that took them up a narrow cleared road high into the mountains. The snow each side of the road was twelve feet high.

The coach climbed slowly up until they were looking down

Author on "Saga Rose"

on a frozen lake, which, although it was iced over, was light blue in colour, It was so cold and high up, the lake was frozen for eleven months of the year, a silent blue and white wonderland.

He also booked a flight on a seaplane, which took off in a fiord by the side of the ship, but was boarded after a boat and enjoyable jeep ride to the other side of the fiord. It really surprised him and the three lady passengers when they set eyes on the seaplane, it looked no bigger that a Dinky toy. One lady, who booked the trip for herself and her mother's birthday gift, whispered to him.

"Oh dear, I hope I've done the right thing, if mother doesn't enjoy the flight I will never hear the end of it."

The third lady told the pilot she wanted the best viewing seat in the front. He told her I would sit there. After helping the old birthday lady board we set off, picking up speed as we passed the Saga Rose. The front compartment had dual controls, which were the size and shape of horseshoes. He felt a bit panicky when the pilot, who had a wicked sense of fun, informed the three ladies in the back,

Seaplane

"The reason I wanted this gentleman sitting in the front is simple, if anything happens to me he can take over the controls." At the same time he grinned and winked to his trainee co-pilot.

As they left the water heading for a mountain, it did not seem possible that the frail little plane, with its slow rate of climb, could clear the top. After a few heart-fluttering moments, they cleared the top to see the vast view below.

They flew around for over an hour, sweeping low over a gigantic glacier, then climbing steeply to clear the mountain before the descent into the fiord. When they landed, and were taxi-ing to the wooden landing stage, he asked the old lady if she was all right.

"Wonderful," she replied. "That is the best birthday present I have ever had." Her daughter's face lit up with delight.

The Saga Rose left the fiords to cruise the coast of Norway with a visit to the lovely old seaport of Bergen and other scenic spots.

THAILAND

This was another great holiday. We spent a week in Bangkok at the Royal River Hotel, with sightseeing trips to some of the hundreds of Buddha temples and The Grand Palace. The Golden Temple with a solid gold statue weighing over five tons. The huge reclining Buddha lying on its side, covered in gold leaf with mother of pearl designs on its feet, has to be seen to be believed. As you walk down the side of it a steady tinkling sound comes from the other side, as pilgrims and visitors drop small coins into tin pots that line the length of the reclining Budda.

A thrilling ride in a narrow long tail speedboat through the marshes, passing villages built on stilts, to the Floating Market of small boats was another highlight. He also liked to wander around on his own visiting the local fish, meat and animal markets, which was an eye opener to say the least.

At night, he visited the kareoke bars with a Scottish couple who became great friends. John Morrison and his wife Aileen were a fun loving couple with his own sense of humour.

They then flew North, a two and a half hours flight, for a fortnight's stay at the Mae Ping Hotel sometimes used by the Thai Royal Family. The hotel had large well-maintained gardens, which housed a traditional Thai theatre and an open-air restaurant with a big stage for those who liked something more modern. If you fancied a change from the hotel's several first class restaurants, you could enjoy a barbecue meal with free entertainment outside. There was also the famous Saga party nights where the wine flowed freely, with reps Kay and Amanda making sure everything ran smoothly.

Across the street from the hotel was the last thing you

expected to see, a bar and massage parlour called, of all things, 'Charlie's.' The owner was a really nice gentleman from Blackpool who had travelled the world before settling here in Chiang Mai.

At the time, Robbie's knee was playing up as it did now and then from 30 years playing football and rugby. Aileen was suffering from backache and John was in the mood for some fun. They all booked massages, which were very popular with the over 50s, most of whom suffered from minor aches and pains, if not worse. The day before, John had been making fun of Dang, Charlie's heavily built Thai wife as she fed him like a baby at the small bar. The massage parlour was air-conditioned with curtained cubicles and judo-type tops and bottoms supplied. The three of them were in adjoining cubicles. John was in for the shock of his life, Dang was hell-bent on revenge. As he lay on his tummy awaiting a soothing massage, Dang changed places with the slim, dainty massage girl and jumped on his back, twisting his arms up his back, and giving the roughest massage he was ever likely to have.

He screamed to Aileen in the next cubicle, who didn't know what was going on, "Help! Help! She's ruddy well killing me."

Aileen told him to shut up and she hoped the girl made a good job of it.

After ten minutes, a grinning Dang gave him a good slap on the rump and left him to the tender mercies of the massage girl. The staff and waiting customers were in tears of laughter at the banter that followed, and a rumpled John crawled out of the cubicle in half pretend agony. He had the gift of getting people out of their shells to let themselves go and enjoy life. Robbie had feet and knee massage, after which he felt like he was walking on air.

An included trip to an elephant camp proved to be better than anyone could have expected. It was in the scenic countryside of Mae Tang. After a demonstration of the elephants' skill and strength one of them kneeled down for a photo session as you sat on its leg. The hide was very soft, and it was like sitting on a cushion. The animals were then taken to a nearby river by their handlers, who were called Mahoots, for a bath and scrub. The Mahoots sat on the elephant's backs and sides as they stood or lay in the water. It was lovely to watch them all enjoying the early morning dip.

A wooden seat with a safety bar was strapped to the elephant's backs. The holidaymakers boarded the animals, which carried two and the Mahoot from a platform on stilts. The elephants splashed down the river before climbing up into the hills.

On the way, they stopped at a hut on stilts to buy bunches of bananas. The elephants stretched their trunks over the heads of the Mahoots, who sat behind their floppy ears to pick the fruit from your hand.

When they got off the elephants, carts driven by pairs of oxen were waiting to take them into the hill villages. You saw how people lived and could purchase clothes made on old-fashioned handlooms. The finished clothes were on coathangers made from branches and twigs.

One of the highlights of the trip was a visit to a village school sponsored by Saga Holidays. The children ran to greet them, taking them by the hand to show them round their school.

Later, they lined up in a dusty play area to entertain their visitors, singing many songs including, 'Twinkle, Twinkle Little Star,' and 'Nick Knack Paddy Whack, give the Dog a Bone.' Some of the lady visitors were in tears as they said goodbye. The oxen carts took them back for the journey to the river on the elephants. At the river were a number of rafts, which held four people and a man with a long pole to guide it along. Once they had to get out of them to avoid a stretch of fast moving white water, walking through the trees and tropical plants before getting in the rafts again. It was a great day out.

A visit to Paradise Gardens, or as it is known locally, Krisada Dai, was a completely different experience. Set in ten acres of the Dai Put National Park in a colourful layout of gardens, streams, quaint wooden bridges and waterfalls. The beautiful wooden buildings blended into the background of tree covered hills giving you a feeling of solitude and peace.

Robbie found on his travels that most people were friendly and helpful. When you read the newspapers sometimes, they could make you too frightened to leave your own backyard.

The coach drove NorthWest to the infamous Bridge over the River Kwai. Thousands of allied prisoners and Thai civilians died from starvation, disease and brutality, at the hands of the Japanese Imperial Army, building it during the Second World War. It was time to think of human's cruelty to their own kind as they took a trip in an old wooden carriage with steam belching engine, for an hour, before being picked up by their coach farther along the railway line.

SAFARI IN KENYA

John Morrison rang to tell him that he and Aileen had booked the safari, giving flight dates and times. Robbie wished them a great holiday but he could not afford to join them. Without telling them he booked the same holiday.

Five months later, he saw them in a restaurant at Heathrow Airport and sat down with them as they read their newspapers. Aileen looked up and stared at him in amazement.

"What are you doing here?"

John looked up with a startled look. After they got over the shock, it was a great reunion. They agreed that if the safari were half as interesting and as much fun as Thailand, it would be money well spent.

They arrived in Nairobi at eight in the morning. The half an hour coach trip to the hotel for an overnight stay took twice as long, as they got caught up in rush hour traffic. It was raining and thousands of people were also walking to work along muddy pathways of red coloured soil, which were separated from the vehicle packed road, by waterfilled ditches. The workers stopped by the ditches to clean their shoes before going in to work.

Robbie's holiday started badly, his dodgy knee from 30 years playing rugby and football was giving him some pain.

After an afternoon sightseeing, he went to bed for a nap. After dinner, he and the Morrison's walked to the beer garden where they spent the evening talking with two charming Kenyan ladies, who said they were biology teachers. As they were leaving early in the morning for the daylong trip to go on safari, they went to bed early. He did not sleep very well because of his knee. When he limped into the dining room for breakfast, a concerned Aileen was very sympathetic, while he and John saw the funny side of going on safari with a peg leg.

The safari party of 35 boarded the five jeeps, which were roomy and comfy. The roofs could be raised, leaving a large gap all round, so you could view the animals and photograph them in the safety of the jeep.

They were introduced to the two people sharing their jeep. One was a retired solicitor who was married to very rich Hungarian lady. She did not fancy a safari and had gone on a world cruise instead. Lucky for some! He was good company, and his knowledge on any place or subject that you cared to mention was incredible.

The other was a pretty Japanese lady who looked a bit young for an over 50s holiday. With her permission, they called her Okie Koky as her real name was too much of a mouthful. She was a hypochondriac, who carried with her a vast array of make-up, wipes, throat sprays, hand creams and medicines, and several pairs of yellow gloves. She always put on a pair before touching anything.

One couple was missing from their jeep through illness. They hoped to catch up and join the group later. Their driver for the trip, Makelele, was a powerfully built man with an ever-smiling face. They would not be roughing it much, only one camp was tented. Makelele told them he hoped to show them the big five in the wild elephants, lions, wildebeest, and the two big cats, which were difficult to sight, leopards and cheetahs.

Once out the city, the roads were very bad, but the jeeps had specially built chassis to take the strain. They passed many townships on the way, made up of dowdy wooden sheds, with colourful names such as Paradise Hotel. The White House, Bar and Butchers and Supermarket. There were very few cars on the roads only lorries. A few people had old bicycles, which were kept in sparkling condition by their owners.

THE TENTED CAMP

The main buildings were made of stone, only the living quarters were tented. The tents were the size of a large bedroom in two parts, the first held two single beds and a wardrobe, and the second held a toilet and shower. You could even order early morning tea.

The large waterhole was separated from the camp by a five-foot trench and electric fence. At night, you ate dinner in the plush restaurant, eating gourmet type meals while watching the many types of animals around the floodlit waterhole.

Although they were near the Equator, it turned cold at night.

As he hobbled back to his tent on the first night, he could hear the scurrying of unseen animals. They had been told to make sure their tents were properly zipped up to stop any of the smaller animals getting in. He got a pleasant surprise when he got into bed; it held two hot water bottles. Thanks to them, his knee was a lot better in the morning.

On the main road to their next camp, they passed many baboons walking along it. Many were carrying babies and would wait until the last second before snatching them from under the wheels, it was frightening, they seemed to be playing a dangerous game with the traffic.

THE TREETOPS HOTEL

The original hotel was built in a tree. The Queen was staying at it as Princess Elizabeth when she heard of her father's death. It was burnt down many years ago by Mau Mau terrorists. Its replacement is made of wood, and built by a waterhole on wooden stilts. They stopped on the way to pick up a soldier armed with a rifle. He guarded them, as they crossed grazing land on foot to the hotel, followed by a herd of buffalo.

From a distance the building didn't look much with its weather-beaten wood, but inside it was really nice, with a wide walkway around the top where you could sit and watch the animals down below. In the middle of the night, an alarm in your room would tell you if there were any lions visiting the waterhole for their supper. The Treetops was only for a short stay. The next two camps were long stay, to go out in the jeeps morning and late afternoon for over two hours at a time, covering large areas of land, to see the varied wildlife that lived there.

On the trip, they came upon a pride of lions lying with swollen stomachs from a zebra kill. They took no notice of the jeep, knowing it was no threat to them. They saw and took photos of many elephants, giraffes, rhinos, different types of deer, dens of hyenas, and bat eared foxes that made their home under a termite mound. They also were lucky enough to see a great herd of wildebeest on the gallop across the Masai Mara. At a river crossing of migrating wildebeest, large crocodiles basked in the sun on the banks waiting on the thunder of hooves, telling them their next meal was on the way. Farther down, a group of hippos lay half-submerged in the river.

The sighting of a leopard, almost invisible as it stalked its prey through long grass and ferns, caused great excitement. Makelele followed the route he thought it was taking for ten minutes or so after it disappeared. He knew his job, it came into full view as it leaped out of its cover on to a fallen tree. It stood perfectly still, looking straight ahead from its vantage point.

The safari jeeps kept in touch by radio. If one spotted a rare animal, the others would drive from miles around to see, photo and admire. Sometimes the vehicles got stuck in the mud, and the nearest would come and tow you out. Towards the end of the safari, a cheetah was seen, half hidden in the grass as it watched a waterhole for the arrival of something tasty.

Okie Koky could be a pain sometimes. She was always the last to turn up for the jeep, walking along as if she had all the time in the world. Makelele would shake his head from side to side and grin.

On one trip they had no sooner left camp when she asked him to stop, she needed to relieve herself. He got out to make sure it was safe before she and her yellow gloves disappeared behind a bush. When John started howling like a hyena, Okie made a breathless return to the jeep. She could also be very sympathetic, and kept asking Robbie how his knee was standing up to the strain of the trip, telling him one day that she was once a professional ice skating dancer, but after a bad knee accident had to give it up. She rolled up the leg of her slacks to show him the scar, John Morrison, with camera at the ready, took a photo of it. Okie Koky was not amused, telling him he was a velly, velly naughty man. After much banter, she joined in the laughter.

LAKE NAKURU

This put the icing on the cake of a truly wonderful holiday. He stayed in a wooden lodge with a balcony overlooking the lake, with nothing to hinder the wonder of it.

It was partly covered in a sea of pink from the thousands of Flamingos on it. Later, they would stand on the shore, near grazing Giraffes and White Rhino, to enjoy the beauty of it all.

The camp itself was protected by a four-foot high electric fence, but the crafty Baboons had found out how to climb over by way of the posts. There were signs warning you not to leave your door open.

When they first arrived he remembered to shut the door, and opened the sliding patio window on the balcony to admire the view. When he went back into the room, he left a half-inch gap in the window. He had no sooner turned his back on it when there was a terrific thump on the balcony. A large Baboon was staring at him with its fingers in the opening. He managed to slam the window shut as the animal pulled its hand away. It gave an angry stare and disappeared.

Okie Koky was not so lucky. She left her door open and a Baboon pinched her malaria tablets and a pair of her precious yellow gloves.

As he walked up to the restaurant the next evening, he came face to face with another one. They both eyed each other suspiciously as they walked passed.

They were no real threat, attack wise, but would not have taken kindly to being patted on the head and called, 'good boy.'

THE TRIBAL VILLAGE

They visited the village of round mud huts surrounded by a hedge of branches and thorns to keep them and their animals safe.

At night, the Cattle and Goats were herded into the empty centre of the village. They were shown many of the tribesmen's skills in hunting, and their famous jumping dance. The men were all slim and healthy looking.

A Cow's neck was pierced to drain blood from it into a jug, this did not harm the Cow, and they drank the blood as part of their diet.

They were allowed to enter a mud hut to see inside. The only item of furniture was a type of small bed, with an open fire. It was dark and cramped, but at the same time warm and cosy. It was hard to believe that people still lived like this and were happy and content.

THE BALLOON SAFARI

It was still dark when they were taken by jeep to the two hot air balloons. The passenger baskets lay on their sides as the ground crew filled the huge balloons that lay on the ground, with hot air from the flaming burners. When they were fully blown up and the baskets upright, they climbed aboard. There were a number of compartments in the baskets to hold around a dozen people and the pilot.

The sun was rising as they soared into the air. The Morrison's were in the other balloon, which changed positions. At times, one would be hundreds of feet in the air, while the other was sweeping low over the heads of the wildlife below. This gave the chance to take great photographs.

After an hour and a half enjoying the wonderful scenery and the thrill of the flight itself, they descended to the ground for a perfect landing, as the basket stayed upright. A slight danger when landing could be caused by a gust of wind catching the balloon and dragging the basket sideways into a termite mound. The back up crew was 24 in number. Jeeps and a tractor followed the flight of the balloons.

Before they took off, John Morrison gave him a bright yellow baseball cap and asked him to try and get a photo of Aileen wearing it.

When showing her daughter photos of the year before in Thailand, her daughter said, "Mum, I'm fed up seeing you in that yellow cap, it seems you have never had it off your head for your last ten holidays!"

Aileen, who had grown very fond of the cap, threw it in the dustbin, but John secretly took it out.

Robbie's balloon was the last to come down. When he

arrived at the food-laden tables for a champagne breakfast beside some trees on the Masai Mara, Aileen was having her photo taken with her balloon pilot, looking smart in his white shirt with gold braid on the shoulders.

He handed her the yellow cap, saying, "Quick, Aileen, put my cap on, I want a photo of you wearing it."

Without as much as a glance she put it on. As she handed it back to him later, a puzzled look crossed her face and she examined it closely. When she saw her grinning husband taking photos to show their daughter, she nearly had a fit, calling him all the names under the sun.

JACK THE LAD

What can a say lads
I've been and done it all
On the Costa Brava
And the Costa Del Sol
I've also been to Rhodes
And the Isle of Kos
Cyprus, Israel and Egypt
Farther afield can also boast.
Everywhere I've sang and danced
With the English rose
Even felt I might have caught
More than just a cold.
Now find the rose a put off
As she staggers from Disco
And with a flip of mini skirt
Bare bum to me she shows.
I'd rather see a class act
Like the one that we all know
Benidorm 'Sticky Vicky'
A legend coast to coast.
She must be a Great Granny now
But she still can see her toes
As she discreetly conjures out
Razor Blades, Flags and Cards
From partly hidden crevice
At early morning shows.

RASTA AND ESTA
SPIT ROAST

Me an ma waman Esta an a vacashan gat inta a situashan. An first day in da sun gat a hunga far grub an fun. Buys a chikan af a da spit, Wak alang with fingas eatan it. Juicas drip dan ma chin onta gold chain an a dan ma front, Estas sun tap getan a stained. Slip inta a Disco bar, lickan fingas, smackan da lips an a spitan da roast. Gatan inta da haladay mood, flashan with da camara. Swigan, gulpan dan da drinks big feet a thampan ta da beat. Esta an da Rum an black starts ta flash har bady parts, than strips dan ta bra an pants. DJ man give as angra tak as ansa ham by cussan back. Bouncer man as eyeballs than ham tak a swing at me. Esta double ham with knee, shuv ham face inta da chikan left an tray. Grab Esta's nick nacks an sun tap, dash with da camara far da exat. Ran dan tha street, dance an, shoutan like two o dem crazy lagar mans. Ma blood na boilan fram al tha excitemant, but Esta gat har glad rags back an. Jump inta da hotel swiman pool, in wet san tap, Esta look real cool. A taks ma waman by da hand, ta relax man an siesta in apartmant.

THE ROOF TOPS

From times gone by they have stood on high, keeping warm and dry all we humans down below. In the middle of the night when the stars are bright they moan and groan, some even walk about.

Chimney Pot croaks out to Aerial, "Look at the mess I'm in, covered in bird droppings for all the World to see."

"You all have seen," shouts Aerial. "The things they do to me they use me as a perch, like branches on a tree and pick at my cable, think a worm they have for tea. I wish they would all fly off to ships far out at sea."

Tile joins in with her high-pitched voice, "I am covered in green moss, mixed up with their droppings, seeds and feather fluff."

"I am fed up," moans Ridge, "At looking down on Tile who needs a brand new face."

"You should be so lucky," growls Gutter underneath. "I am

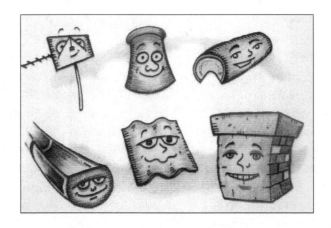

bending under the strain of old bird nests and tufts of grass, it's giving me much pain."

"I am cracking up," wheezes Chimney. "My cement is falling out, the Earthlings with their ladders take no notice of my plight. One hundred years I have stood up here watching the street below, how fresh and bright we were back then when Tile's face was clean and glowed."

"Yes," said Ridge, "She was lovely then but now her age does show."

"It's not my fault," shrills Tile, "My face had no cover, hailstones and rain batter it, I cannot change the weather."

Gutter growled with a groan, "I am filled up to the brim, if I'm not emptied soon the strain will do me in. We shelter all these Earthlings and keep them warm and dry, but rarely do they think of us who live near to the sky."

Chimney, with his creaking old joints, wheezed wearily, "I don't think I can support Pot and Aerial on my head and shoulders for much longer if I don't get my wounds repaired, in fact, we are all well past our selling date."

"Speak for yourself," piped up Aerial. "I am young and fit with a long life in front of me."

"What a silly young fool you are," wheezed Chimney angrily. "You are lucky to have lived this long, with all these new Satellite Dishes and underground cables for Television, it's a wonder you were not taken off my shoulder years ago."

They all went silent for a while, shocked by old Chimney's outburst. Aerial and Pot felt guilty, they knew that they were a heavy burden on him.

Ridge tried to cheer them all up. "Do you remember when we were all young? And the street was made of cobblestones that never wore out, even though horse driven and hand-pulled carts rattled and bumped along it all day long. The baker, a big round jolly man who the children called Dumpling, and his big white horse called, Nobbin, who always had a nosebag on to munch it's oats from. Milly, the milk woman with her little donkey and cart that carried a big churn of creamy fresh milk to sell door to door. Nobody locked their door and the Earthlings borrowed bread, jam and sugar off each other, to keep them from going hungry until pay-day. The children collecting horse dung off the street with buckets and shovels then spreading it on the gardens to make the vegetables strong and healthy. The horse drawn cartloads of coal, which were dumped onto the cobbles for the young lads to wheelbarrow to the back yard coal sheds. Some of the lumps of coal were so large it took two lads to lift one. On Saturday mornings little girls would have their jobs to do, cleaning windows, polishing brass doorplates, washing and scrubbing the front doorsteps and fetching the groceries from the street's corner shop. They would moan in the street about having to clean the large iron fire range, which was used for heating the water, and cooking, with a polish called, black lead, they said it made a mess of their hands. Do you remember the Lamplighter who went along the street every night with a long pole with a hook on it to light the gas mantle in the street lights?"

"I liked it then," shrilled Tile, as they all watched a Fox and its two cubs drinking out of one of the many potholes in the street.

"But the Earthlings do some silly things now. Why did they cover the cobbles up with that smelly black stuff called Tarmac, which is always having to be patched up?"

"Ah," croaked Pot, "That was when all the cars and lorries started to fill the street day and night, long before the ugly street humps we have now, to slow the traffic."

"That is what I mean," replied Tile, "The cobbles would slow the traffic down and they look better and don't wear out."

They all nodded their heads in agreement and were surprised that Tile could be so clever, they had always thought she was a bit of a dimwit.

"I would like to see the children playing in the street again," said Ridge. "With their skipping rope games, or playing hop, skip and jump on the pavements, laughing and giggling or crying when they played tricks on each other."

"I remember when Mr. Snout kept pigs in his back yard," croaked Pot. "No food was wasted then and because their parents could not afford a proper football the lads used a pig's bladder instead."

"They also caused a lot of trouble when they took apples off the trees, and trampled on some of the potato and other plants when they played hide and seek in the back gardens," grumbled Gutter. "I liked them better when they were indoors or playing marbles on the pavements. Do you remember the time when the only people who had a car were doctor Sinclair and Mr. Scargoyle who was the manger of the coalmine? The Mr. Beckham who lived at house number seven was trapped for two days under a fall of coal down the mine. They brought him home in a coal cart because there was no ambulance."

"Yes, I remember," croaked Pot, "You could tell which men worked down the coalmine, they had blue scars on their faces."

"What made the scars and why were they blue?" asked Aerial, for this was before his time.

"When they were hacking with a pick at the coalface, sharp chips of coal cut their faces, coal dust got into the wounds and turned them blue."

"How do you know that?"

"Because, Aerial, Mr, Scargoyle held a meeting in the street, right under our noses and talked about the mess the miners faces and lungs were in, from the coal dust."

"The coal fires spoilt the old days for me," wheezed Chimney, between coughs, "I was smoking non stop, apart from when my inside was being cleaned, for year after year. I used to hate it when the chimney sweep cleaned me out with a big round brush, which was fixed to a long pole. I was in agony for days afterwards. The brush got stuck in poor old Pot once and nearly knocked him off my head. I think Pot has a croaky voice now because of all the black coal smoke that used to belch out of his head and block out the sun. I hope they never fire me up again, the smoking would finish me off and Pot would lose his voice forever. I like the street a lot better now, it is not so noisy and even some cars help by parking both sides of the street corners to stop those long rumbling lorries thundering along the street. The Earthlings are also a lot more pleasant to look at, now they have lost the pale look on their faces from working long hours in sweaty factories and underground. I like to see all the bright colourful clothes they wear now and those shoes they call trainers, some of which have funny names on them. In the old days they all dressed more or less the same. The only time they really looked smart was when they wore what they called their, Sunday best, for weddings, funerals and going to Church. With the men in their one smart suit, bowler hat, instead of a flat cap, white shirt with a starched collar, a tie, which was usually black, as was their only pair of shoes.

Some of them proudly owned waistcoats with large pocket watches on chains displayed in the pockets. They would walk arm in arm with their wives who were dressed in long skirts with petticoats underneath, white blouses with coats or short jackets on top. In the summer you could see their shoes as they all wore the same length dresses, which reached halfway down their legs.

It's a good job they all wore different hats of all shapes and sizes when dressed in their Sunday best or we would not have been able to tell them apart from up here."

"Those were the days of Kate the Tinker, with her horse and cart piled high with second-hand clothes. The women in the street would jostle each other as they crowded around the cart to buy what they needed for a few pennies," croaked Pot. "It was said that the Tinker got the clothes from a hospital where people did not need them anymore."

After all the years of not being looked after by the Earthlings they had sheltered for so long, Tile and Ridge could now move about as all their joints had become free. Even Pot could move about a little on top of Chimney.

One clear night with the full moon shining bright Tile climbed carefully up the Roof to sit with her best friend Ridge. They had been planning for a long time to visit down below. This could only happen with the help of Chimney who had become bossy and grumpy in his old age and easily upset by all

143

his aches and pains. As Tile walked up the Roof she was spotted by Ginger Tom, the most feared cat in the street. He had just come out of the back garden of Mr. and Mrs Skintight, in the row of terraced houses opposite. Clamped and wriggling in its jaws was a not very happy mouse, an unwelcome present for Ginger's owners, the Plump family whom the Roof Tops now sheltered.

The mouse disappeared down the nearest street drain as the cat's mouth dropped open from surprise and shock of seeing Tile moving about on the Roof. In a state of panic Ginger bolted across the street and dived through its catflap, slid along the polished wooden hallway and crashed with an almighty bang into the far wall. The noise awakened the Plump family, thinking they were being burgled Mr. Plump lumbered downstairs from the bedroom clutching his alarm clock for protection. When he saw the dazed Ginger Tom he said,

"Oh dear, whatever have you been up to now?"

At the same time he looked around uneasily to see if Ginger had brought another one of his many different gifts home.

The Plumps were big football fans, Mr. Rooney Plump supported Manchester United but his wife Fergie was mad keen on Manchester City. This caused a lot of arguments between them. Their daughter, Dotty, didn't know whether she was coming or going, she went with her dad one week to watch the United play and the next week with her mum to the City. They were as different as chalk and cheese from their best friends across the street, the Skintight's, who did everything together, some people even said that they were joined at the hip.

Monty and Olive Skintight had no children of their own and spoiled Dotty Plump, treating her as if she was their daughter. They were from Scotland and spent all their holidays there, playing and watching golf. Olive Skintight was so small and slim her husband, Monty, could carry her around the golf course when she got tired after the first nine holes or so, in his golf club bag. The two families often ate at each other's homes. The Skintight's ate only fresh fruit, vegetables and fish at home, but when they felt a little run down they would visit the Plumps who loved a big fry up, chip butty's, cream cakes and fizzy drinks. The Plumps when they felt bloated and tired from eating too much would eat at the Skintight's. This strange diet stopped the Plump parents from getting plumper and the Skintight's from losing any more weight. Sad to say, it was not doing Dotty any good that even though she did not eat a lot was becoming plumper every day.

It was a worrying time for the RoofTops. Chimney had been pleased when he stopped smoking for good. He felt a lot better and he was really proud that the Earthlings liked his fireplace so much they didn't brick it up. He could hear from the fireplace everything that was happening down below, he would then tell the others so they could have a good gossip.

A few days before bonfire night, which the RoofTops loved as they were all lit up by fireworks, there was a large gathering of Earthlings in the Plump's house. Aerial worked overtime all night as his antenna and cable passed a signal to the television in the Plump's sitting room. The Earthlings were watching, amongst other things a powerful man named Barack Obama who said he was going to do away with the old and rebuild from new. The RoofTops had good reason to be worried by this. All around them they could see rows of old houses being knocked down and replaced by new ones with no chimneys, but strange panels called Solar, instead. There was a glimmer of hope for their survival at the moment, because of something called a credit crunch. The Earthlings were short of money and had stopped building new and were repairing the old. With a bit of luck Tile might even get a facelift.

As Tile sat on top of the Roof with Ridge, all was still and peaceful in the glow of the full moon. Gutter was shaking himself gently as he tried to get rid of some of his rubbish into the street below. Aerial, who was off duty as the television down below had been switched off for the night, was having a quiet chat with Pot about his latest cable attack by a pigeon, and Chimney was chuckling to himself about some happy times in the past. When Ridge saw that old Chimney was in such a good mood he thought it's now or never.

"Chimney," he shouted, "Tile and I would like to make a visit down below, would you please let us climb down your inside?"

"Oh, I don't think that would be wise," wheezed Chimney. "My inside is very poorly now and not very safe, you could also be in great danger from the Earthlings."

"Don't be a spoil sport," shrilled Tile, "We are willing to take the chance and will try to bring you back something nice."

After much pleading and help from the others who urged Chimney to let them go, he agreed. "All right then, but be careful and don't dig your feet too hard into my cracks or poke too deep with your fingers, I am in enough agony as it is. It will be pretty dark as you go down but I will feel where you are and say where the best holds are."

Pot moved from the centre to the side of Chimney's large square head to make room for his daring two friends as they climbed up to join him. Being the heavier of the two, Ridge started the long and dangerous journey down Chimney's dark inside with Tile following close behind. Just before the Earthlings had stopped firing him up Chimney had been swept, this helped the two friends a lot as only a few small pieces of Chimney's inside fell into the fireplace far below. This made Chimney gasp for breath as his voice guided them safely down. Ridge and Tile hugged with joy and relief when they finally reached the bottom. They stopped to rest for a while and listen to hear if they had disturbed any of the Earthlings. All was quiet as they pushed a firescreen to one side and the light from the full moon flooded into the fireplace from the undrawn, curtained windows.

Curious at the noise of bits falling down the Chimney a

silent Ginger Tom was waiting to greet them. They froze in terror as it stared them in the face, its fur standing on end, back arched, hissing and spitting at them. As it raised a paw to strike them Ridge whispered to Tile out of the corner of his mouth,

"When I count to two shout, boo, as loud as you can." The sudden yell from the two strangers startled the cat and it turned tail and fled across the room and up the stairs.

"Phew, that was a close call," said a trembling Ridge.

"Don't I know it," stuttered Tile. "I have seen what that ball of fur does to mice and other creatures, including cats, in the middle of the night."

"Not to worry," whispered Ridge. "I don't think he will risk one of his nine lives on us again."

Shaken by their narrow escape with Ginger Tom they stepped warily into the Plump's front room. They found it hard to believe that the Earthlings lived so comfortably, a thick pile carpet covered the floor, with nice chairs and sofas to sit on.

In a corner was a big flat screen with a black surround, standing on a matching black glass table.

"That must be a television," whispered Ridge excitedly. "Look, Aerial's cable is fixed to the back, how happy he will be to know how well it looks with no bird droppings or peck marks on it."

As they made their way to the open kitchen door and passed the bottom of the stairs, they both stopped in fright, a loud rumbling noise was coming from upstairs. It would stop for a time then start up again like a roll of thunder. After a while, shaking with fear they moved on, thinking it must be a normal noise in the Earthlings house. They were right; it was Dotty's parents snoring their heads off. From the doorway of the kitchen, in the dim light from the moon, they could see a fridge, standing next to a washing-up sink and draining board with a curtained off space underneath, a cooker and fitted floor cupboards with a wooden worktop.

They were looking to see what was behind the curtain when

they heard the stairs creaking eerily. As they peeped out from their hiding place in the waste bin's space behind the curtain, a round white blob appeared in the kitchen doorway. When the round shape opened the fridge door and the light from inside shone out, the daring RoofTops gave a sigh of relief. It was not a ghost, but Dotty Plump in a long white nightgown, walking in her sleep.

With her eyes closed tight she stuffed the goodies from the fridge into her mouth, groaning with pleasure as she munched. Unknown to Dotty or her parents this was the reason she kept getting plumper. Her mother had noticed food going missing from the fridge and had asked Dotty if it was her who was taking it. This had made Dotty angry and she said she knew nothing about it, which was true. As her mother knew that Dotty never told lies she thought it must be her husband, Rooney, having the odd fattening snack between meals. After she had eaten her fill Dotty, still in dreamland, smacked her lips and made her way back up the creaking stairs to bed.

Ridge and Tile left their hiding place and searched in the floor cupboards. They found a number of things that would be useful including a pair of scissors, a ball of string, a bottle of cough mixture and an empty supermarket bag. Unable to see what was on the worktop and sink-draining board above, Tile had a great idea. With help from Ridge she cut a length of string from the ball and tied one end around her middle and climbed up the sink curtain by gripping onto the folds and the thick fabric. She found two spoons and a fork on top, and passed them down to Ridge on the piece of string. When she got down, and after a few moments rest she climbed on Ridge's shoulders opened the fridge door and went inside, dropping what food and fizzy drinks that were left, to Ridge, who put them in the supermarket bag. Before lowering herself down onto Ridge's shoulders she made sure the fridge door was left wide open, to try and help Dotty. If her mum saw the fridge door wide open and empty she might try to find out what was really happening to her daughter.

Tired out after all the thrills and danger they had been through the weary friends dragged the supermarket bag from the kitchen to the fireplace. This took them some time, as the bag was heavy from everything they had collected. They were glad when they reached the safety of the fireplace and pulled the screen into its proper position behind them. They took the scissors and ball of string out of the bag and while Ridge was wiping the sweat off his forehead Tile tied the string around his waist. With Chimney helping him find his way up, Ridge reached the top and was pulled out by a beaming Pot while Aerial and Gutter gave a welcome cheer. Tile cut the string that Ridge had taken up the Chimney from the ball in the fireplace, and tied it tightly around the top to the bag of presents. Pot and Ridge then pulled the bag up. As they had planned Ridge dropped the cut end of string that had been tied around the bag, back down into the fireplace. Tile tied it around her and was safely pulled up to the Roof, to her relieved and now happy family.

The bottle of cough medicine was given to the grateful Chimney and Pot to ease their sore throats and one spoon to Aerial to wave about and scare off nasty pecking birds. Gutter cried with relief and thanks after the two heroes slid down the Roof and cleaned him out with the second spoon and the fork. They then held a big party, eating and drinking, with lots of talk about the great adventure down below. Aerial, feeling very proud about his cable being connected to a smart television kept asking all about it, while Pot and Chimney cleared their throats.

Mrs Fergie Plump got out of her bed bright and early that morning, to do her cleaning. It was a very special day for her, Manchester City was playing at home against top of the premier football league, Manchester United. She and husband Rooney were going to see the game but would sit apart, he in the visitors section of the ground in the red colours of United, while she sat in a sea of light blue colour with the rest of the City supporters. They both took a defeat for their team when they played each other very badly. Dotty never went to these games, as she did not want to upset one parent by going with the other. She stayed with the Skintight's for three or four days until her parents were talking to each other again and being cuddly. Although she missed her parents Dotty loved being spoilt by Monty and Olive Skintight. They had also taught her how to play golf, which she enjoyed and was now pretty good at playing.

Mrs Plump looked down into the fireplace with a puzzled look on her face, wondering how the ball of string and scissors had got there from the kitchen. As she looked down, scratching her head, a piece of greaseproof paper fluttered down the Chimney and landed on top of the string. It was the wrapping off her favourite cream sponge cake now missing from the fridge. That does it, she thought, it's time Rooney climbed up his ladder to see what was happening up on the Roof. She had been asking him to do this for weeks, since two damp patches had appeared on the ceiling of their bedroom.

The fireplace was her second shock that morning, she had already seen the empty fridge in the kitchen and made up her mind to put a stop to whatever was going on, by locking up the fridge at night and not stocking it with so much food.

Up above, the Roof Tops were fast asleep with not a croak, wheeze or cough to be heard, and Gutter, who was now empty and free from pain had a smile on his face instead of a scowl.

Look after all the RoofTops
To keep you warm and snug
Or you will shiver
Damp or wet
From cracks and Gutter stuffed.

WHERE DO I BELONG?

In the Summer of 2005, after spending many months without moving out of the area he lived, Robbie decided to treat himself to Sunday lunch in the village of Anstey, four miles from the City centre. As he sat in a crowded restaurant, he began to feel ill at ease, something was definitely wrong.

For a while he could not think what it was. Suddenly it became clear, there was not a coloured face to be seen. It seemed as if he had moved to a different country and he didn't like it one bit. Leaving his half-eaten meal, he drove back to his mixed up community.

This left him in a troubled state of mind because in 2004 he made up his mind to spend Christmas and New Year in Phutek, Thailand. Some Indian friends advised him to try Goa in India.

After much thought, he went to Goa, an ex Portuguese colony. On arrival, he spent most of his holiday in one of the many beach shacks. The meals were cheap and the people very friendly. It was like home from home. At night, the shack owners took the free sunbeds away and replaced them with candle-lit tables, where you could sit and enjoy music and firework displays.

One morning, a little girl walked along the deserted white sands with two adults, as he sat on his own talking across the sanded floor to the shack owner. They carried with them two long bamboo poles, rope and some other items in a straw basket. The adults, who looked like they were the child's parents, pushed the poles into the sand in front of the shack about thirty feet apart, after tying the rope near the top ends. The rope became tightly held high in the air. Each pole had a platform about the size of an average pancake near the top.

The tiny girl, aged about five, climbed up a pole to stand on the little platform. A water jug as big as herself was raised up to her. Balancing it on her head, she walked along the rope in her bare feet, then back again. She was then thrown a steel ring about twelve inches wide and walked along the rope, turning it with her feet.

While the adults took the pole down, the girl came to him and bowed politely as he placed some coins in the bowl she held out.

What amazed him, besides her uncanny sense of balance, was the fact that he and the shack owner were the only people on the sun-drenched beach. It made him realise that nothing is too much trouble when you don't know where your next mouthful of food is coming from.

The Tsunami hit Phutek that same morning. The Indian friends, who talked him into going to Goa instead, had probably saved his life. What really worried him now was why he felt more at home thousands of miles from Britain, than he did in an English village four miles from his home in the City. Was he losing his identity?

2006

Charles Grimm had led a colourful life. His career in the British Royal Navy as a deep-sea diver and training instructor had taken him into many adventurous and perilous situations. After his service in the Navy he set up his own business, a Scuba diving centre, in the Caribbean.

Charles was a lifelong bachelor but he rarely slept alone. He was six feet two with a slim muscular body, a thick mop of wavy black hair, sparkling blue eyes and gleaming white teeth, which were constantly on display. He would have fitted perfectly as the romantic hero in any Barbara Cartland style novel. Unlike his surname, Charles was a fun loving character with a sense of humour second to none.

With his business thriving and expensive gifts, which were showered on him by beautiful and grateful clients, he became a very rich man. Like many men and women with more money and playthings than makes sense, Charles would sometimes give in to the seedy side of his character and seek the company of elderly ladies of the night. A change from the string of lookalike, and usually boring, spoilt beauties who graced his bed, he needed this change of company to recharge his vitality.

At the age of fifty-five he sold his business and spent many years touring the world. He eventually returned to his homeland to tour and walk the length and breadth of the British Isles.

Nature had been kind to Charles. At sixty-five, with his healthy life style, no stressful family ties or money worries, he was fitter than most men half his age. He decided to settle down for a while to take stock of how he would spend the rest of his life. A small village on England's East Coast had appealed to him on his travels. Chapel-Saint-Leonards was just a few miles from the busy holiday town of Skegness. He booked into the Vine Hotel in the centre of the village. It was late September, the weather was warm and dry but it did turn chilly at night.

On the second night of his stay he took the short walk from the village on to the concrete walkway, six feet above the shoreline. There was a slight breeze and the full moon glinted on the calm sea, Charles felt a deep feeling of contentment as he approached the porch to the small entertainment bar, which stood in isolation next to the walkway. It had been transformed from ladies and gents toilets many years before. The building and interior were unique in character and he had spent a pleasant afternoon there six months previously. With a tiny bar at one end, its long narrow interior was festooned with fishing objects. The cushioned bench seating along each wall was made of highly polished wood, with medium sized beer casks serving as tables.

It not only catered for humans but dogs as well. At the bottom of the large wooden porch extension a free supply of water and doggy snacks were available for doggies on their walkies.

As he reached the bottom step of the porch he knew a night of quiet reflection was not possible. It was kareoke night, a party of middle-aged holidaymakers joining in as a lady gave a fair rendering of the song, 'Maggie May.' After a few beers and Jack Daniel's, he got into the party mood. The jolly crowd was also celebrating the fiftieth birthday of Tim, a loud spoken gent with a shaven head, who had an endearing habit of lifting his T-shirt to proudly show off his beer belly. It was well past midnight when the party left with a long and noisy farewell. Charles stopped behind chatting with the owners, Paul Greaves and Gillian Harrison.

"They were a friendly bunch," he remarked.

Paul smiled as he replied, "Yes, the Chissets love their

booze and a sing song." Gillian nodded her head in agreement.

"Why do you call them, 'Chissets'?" asked a curious Charles.

"Well, they come in their thousands every year to spend their annual holidays. Their homes are situated in the industrial Midlands. Apart from booze and fish and chips, they have gained a reputation locally of being not tight, but very careful when they spend their money."

He continued, "Unlike the Scots their thrift is no myth. The local business people soon realised that no matter how much they enlarged their price tags on goods they would always be asked, "How much is it?" Hence the name Chissets. They are becoming an ethnic minority where they live in the industrial Midlands and are moving to the coasts or the carefree haven of Scotland."

It was two in the morning before Charles staggered back to his hotel. He could have been on the moon, there was not a soul about, not even a stray dog. The hotel was in complete darkness as he inserted the hotel door key in the lock, to his dismay it would not unlock the door. There was no night porter and all the living accommodation was upstairs and, try as he might, he could not arouse anybody. His car keys were in his room or he could have slept in the comfort of his E-Type Jag. Charles had roughed it on many occasions and resigned himself to trying to sleep on one of the hotel's front garden seats. He knew it would be around seven o'clock before anybody came out of the hotel for a stroll, or to get a morning paper.

After twenty minutes on the garden seat, wearing only a silk shirt and lightweight summer trousers, he realised he would have to find somewhere warmer or get a serious cold, or worse. As he walked across the village green, an alley, down the side of the Co-operative store, caught his attention; it might give him some protection from the chilly sea breeze. As he walked down the dark alley he heard a strange noise, luckily for him it was a Generator, blowing out hot air at regular intervals. Searching the alley he found an empty milk crate and sat down on it with his back against the gaps in the fence, which surrounded the Generator. Every now and then he would stand up, turn around, and enjoy the blast of hot air on his front it was sheer bliss. He chuckled to himself as he saw the funny side to his predicament. He had slept in some of the best hotels in the world, and now he was locked out of a hotel in a sleepy English village, sitting like a tramp, with the warm embrace of a Generator as a partner.

He had never felt so grateful to a night's companion in his life. Between dozing off occasionally he thought about his future and an ambition he wished to accomplish. At half past six he made his way to the local Spar shop to pass the time and buy a paper.

Janet Smith's heart missed a beat as she looked up from the morning papers, she was busily putting in their racks. There was something about the rather dishevelled and slightly shivering Charles that attracted her to him.

"Really sir, you should have put on a jacket or something warm on a chilly morning like this."

Charles was thankful for the slim, elderly lady's concern about him. He grinned as he told her how he had spent the last few hours. Janet was amazed that this man could be cheerful rather than angry about his ordeal. She warmed to him even more as they chatted like old friends. Charles invited the widow, Janet, to join him for dinner at the hotel the following evening.

He got into the hotel just after seven o'clock and slept soundly until lunchtime. After checking his key in the lock, the hotel staff was most apologetic and cut his bill by half. After lunch as he sat at the hotel bar having a drink, a hand clasped his shoulder. It was Tim, the birthday man and his wife, the Maggie May singer. He told them about the Generator blowing hot air. It was to be an embarrassing mistake. In his loud voice

Tim shouted to his brother Tom, at the other end of the room,
"Hey Tom, Charles has just had the longest blow job ever!"

After an enjoyable dinner with Janet their friendship blossomed. He settled down with her in the village and achieved his ambition, to write articles on his travels and diving experiences.

At weekends they joined parties of Chissets, in the Admiral Benbow beach bar or the Vine Hotel, to enjoy their company at Pauline's and Lols Starfinders Kareoke. When he went out on his own he made sure he had a spare key to Janet's bungalow, her snug bedroom and warm body made the Generator cold in comparison.

FRED GAMBLES
2008

Samantha Silk, or 'Hot Totty' as she was known to her male colleagues, pulled the collar of her coat up to her chin in a vain attempt to keep herself warm. It was a beautiful night, but there was a definite chill in the air. She shook her head slightly and a crescendo of blonde curls fell across her face blocking her vision. Pushing her tresses impatiently out of her eyes, she sighed softly and looked up at the sky. Samantha had never seen anything that looked more awesome. There was a full moon shimmering silently above her and a smattering of stars sparkling like diamonds displayed on a cloak of black velvet. She was so caught up in her appreciation of its beauty, she almost didn't catch the subtle rustling in the bushes to her far left. With churning stomach and cold perspiration trickling down her face, she slowly turned to view the bushes and walked hesitantly towards them.

As a young, desk bound police woman, her blonde hair and slim but curvy figure had thrust her into this plain clothes duty as bait for a serial molester. The fiend had been creating terror in suburbs of the city for over a year. The only clue to the molester was notes stuck in the victim's backs, with the words in capitals, FRED THE SHRED, in red ink. The victims were attacked at random, from Samantha look-alike, to pensioners, children with bank accounts, and a young man with bleached blonde hair and a feminine walk.

Samantha Silk was following a family tradition by joining the Force. Her grandfather had been a Force legend in his time. An old fashioned beat bobby, he had controlled his patch by knowing all the locals by name and their varied religions. After a few clips around the ears and on rare occasions a kick up the rear, from an early age, the youths on his beat respected him and his uniform. The co-operation of parents who in those days were all ardent supporters of, 'Spare the rod, spoils the child' had made his job much respected and pleasant to dispatch.

As Samantha approached the bushes the smell of hot curry swept over her and her heart skipped a beat. Suddenly a fox darted from the undergrowth across her feet with the leftovers of an Indian takeaway clamped in its jaws. Shaking from shock she hoped that her back up of one, part time policeman was near at hand for quick assistance if needed. Her feet were already aching from the high-heeled shoes she had been asked to wear by her superiors, as these appeared to be another of the molester's fetishes.

As she continued her lonely walk she thought of her ambition to be a member of the 'Family Car Control Force,' the S.A.S. of the uniformed branch. A successful capture of the molester would speed her to this goal and a career in a comfortable police car. Because of suspicion in the Force that the molester somehow seemed aware, on previous attempts to catch him or possibly her, of police movements, Samantha was not allowed radio contact with her back up, this made her feel very vulnerable. She was grateful that the moonlight gave her some protection. Except for city centre headquarters, all police stations in a ten-mile radius were closed due to a lack of funding. 'The thin blue line' of police, like a protected species was rarely seen.

Thousands of people would turn up at sporting events hoping to catch a glimpse of them, and many children grew up believing that all police personnel were legless, because they only saw the top half of their bodies as they passed by in Panda cars. At that very moment, thousands of Panda cars and their crews all over the country were discreetly hidden near main roads. Their main priority, to keep a bleary eye open for 'Speed Camera Fanatics.' This growing band of tormented people were now a threat to government funding. Thousands of Speed Cameras were being stolen or destroyed on the spot.

As Samantha reached the first of the densely populated 'Road Hump' streets, now eerily quiet, she became very tense. No one in their right mind now walked on the pavements of 'Road Hump' streets after midnight.

This had come about after protesters started digging up the suspension ruining, exhaust spewing of fumes, and jolting of disabled passengers caused by council 'Road Humps.' The local council at great expense quickly replaced them. After a while the protesters had realised they were making a grave error of judgement. As the 'Road Humps' were so close together they decided it would be easier to tarmac in between them, creating a level surface once again. The council in their wisdom rebuilt the 'Humps' on top. With both sides unwilling to give in, the streets were now four feet higher than the pavements. The shadowed pavements now hid a multitude of general low life, human and pests. Tarmac became a scarce commodity, travelling families unable to buy their main source of income, turned to crime. Some of them in desperation raided isolated farmhouses to trap roosting House Martins and Pigeons to devour, also stealing anything they could find at the risk of being unlawfully shot.

Suddenly Samantha saw in the distance the head and shoulders of a lone figure, its shoulders hunched against the cold night air. As the figure drew nearer a shiver of fear ran down her spine, it appeared to be wearing what looked like a loose fitting, ankle length black dress. In contrast its head shone like a beacon in the moonlight making it impossible to distinguish its features. At that moment Samantha was glad she had kept on her regulation police underwear, complete with suspenders. Tucked securely in her right suspender was the comforting feeling of her 'Panda Protective Stiletto.' She was as pure as the driven snow and many of her future Panda car male partners would swear to the Stiletto's sharpness.

Samantha relaxed and smiled as the 'sinister' looking figure approached her. It was the parish priest in flowing cassock, his baldhead shining, and his best selling book in hand. He was returning from the Swallow pub, in the nearby village of Thurnby, after a late night sermon there, on the evils of drink. After a short chat he went on his way, swaying unsteadily from side to side.

As she left the 'Road Hump' streets off the Portway Road it was a relief to walk on a level pavement again. She made her way to what was once a busy police station but was now a council rent arrears office. At the back of the building a hut was still used by Panda car patrols for a well-earned cuppa and to relax until their shift was over. Samantha was looking forward to making herself a nice strong cup of tea. Waiting in the shadows of the empty hut was an agitated figure wearing face make up, and a blonde wig.

Fred Gamble had served the community for many years as a loyal and trusted Bank Manager, looking after customer's deposits and mortgage loans as if they were his own. He appreciated his well-paid job and the esteem in which clients held him. To give something back to society he became a volunteer Special Constable in the Police Force, in his spare time. There was a dramatic change in his personality during the credit crunch in 2008, when his failing Bank was merged with another and he lost his job. The shock of this, and his pent up anger at his Bank superiors awarding themselves huge sums of money for losing shareholders hard earned money, caused him to have a nervous breakdown.

During this time his wife of many years became puzzled as to why her tights and undies became stretched and baggy for no apparent reason. She had been using the same British brand most of her adult life with no problems. It all became clear when she caught her startled husband cross-dressing in her underwear. Betty Gamble had found it very hard to deal with her husband's mood swings and disruptive behaviour since he lost his job, and this discovery was too much for her to take. Shaking her bleached blonde head in disbelief she told Fred to leave the family home. Alone in a dingy bedsit Fred Gamble's other self became an obsession. The daring and dangerous Transvestite, as he called her, gradually became the dominant side of the staid ex Bank Manager's character. Fred Gamble knew from his police contacts of Samantha Silk's route that night.

He had taken the precaution of sending an urgent message by radio to Samantha's back up, P.C. Ian Blair, supposedly from Police Headquarters, sending him on a wild goose chase to apprehend two burly men acting suspiciously in an unmarked car.

The first Samantha knew of her attacker's presence was an arm tightly encircling her neck from behind, dragging her deeper into the shadows. Her molester was muttering dire threats if she dared to resist. As he pawed at her breasts with his free hand, the smell of Chanel perfume and Garlic breath against her cheek made her senses reel. With the ever-tightening arm across her throat, she felt herself slipping into a dark, bottomless pit. She wriggled frantically to reach up her skirt and managed to grasp her Panda Protective Stiletto. With a twisting motion she stabbed backward into her molester's groin. With her legs like jelly she gasped for breath as Gamble released his stranglehold and collapsed, screaming in agony, half castrated.

Samantha kicked off her shoes and stumbled towards a 'Road Hump' street, seeking help. From a vantagepoint on top of a 'Hump' she saw a convoy of lights in the distance. Fifty Panda cars were heading towards her as they returned from 'Speed Camera' patrol. She sank to her knees from shock and relief; the bloody Stiletto still clutched in her hand.

A few years later, after a series of free operations on the National Health Service, a Transvestite Gamble was front-page news in the National newspapers as she partied happily with a host of Britain's most notorious criminals in Broadmoor Mental Prison.

By coincidence, at the same time a newly promoted Police Sergeant Samantha Silk, was on full pay compassionate leave, from the 'Family Car Control Force.' While her five million pounds claim for racial discrimination and prejudice against the Muslim Chief of Police, for being passed over for quicker promotion, and his attitude towards her free flowing blonde hair, was settled.

A COMEDY OF POLITICS
2011

Jaws Brown had started his working life with good intentions, in the manufacturing industry, but with no job security and rip off pension schemes, he could only see a bleak future ahead of him. A non-productive job in the government, or with the council was the answer, with more job security and inflation proof pension. The trouble was, most of the population had come to this conclusion. Plus hordes of legal and illegal immigrants were having to be found secure employment first, to supplement free social benefits they had not contributed to. Brown took exception to this and decided with many more to milk the benefit system. He was living a life of luxury, fiddling with large sums of money, when greed and his ego got the better of him, number ten led to his downfall. He started claiming income support for ten non-existing families and incapacity benefits for ten husbands with back twinges. A suspicious benefits employee interrogated Brown's closest friends and neighbours, Cherry Blair and her husband who Brown, on an impulse, had confided in. Reluctantly they broke their promise to tell no one and betrayed him. He was found guilty of fraud and false pretences and sentenced to one month in prison with three weeks off for good behaviour.

In the open prison he met a conman, Nick Cleggs, who taught him the tricks of his trade. Nick had fooled many with promises of a richer and better future. After his release, Brown conned his way around Britain. His main earnings area was The Kingdom of Fife, stretching from the Firth of Forth river to St. Andrews up the east coast. One of his biggest and most beneficial con tricks was selling the Firth of Forth road bridge to a rich, influential American, Obama Palin. The tourist was convinced by his plausible story that the bridge was by its sell by date and could be shipped in sections, when a vehicle tunnel was completed under the Firth of Forth.

Obama was also convinced it was a genuine deal, for he was aware that the British, for some unknown reason, were selling off their prize assets and heritage to the European Union and beyond.

The thought of going to prison for his crimes did not bother Brown, who had served a few short spells inside. The days of slopping out their body fluids were long gone. With a variety of food available, three quality meals a day, Christmas dinner and celebrations, Easter eggs, leisure facilities, E.U. controlled human rights to sue the taxpayers at every opportunity. He treated these interludes as stress rests. Practically anything you wanted could be smuggled in. Female visitors were greeted with open arms. With condom filled goodies hidden in various orifices, searches were a rarity; the human rights lawyers would have rubbed their hands together with glee in anticipation of another long drawn out, lucrative court case.

After being falsely accused of assault on a woman who called him a bigot and serving time, Brown's prison holidays were about to be interrupted. Pensioners living on paltry basic pensions all over Britain were about to be seen and heard, in a National revolt against their shabby treatment by the Government, Social Services and the National Health Service. Pensioners in Scotland on their starvation diet of mince and tatties were on the move. In England, active wrinklies were wheeling frail pensioners out of hospital corridors who were suffering from neglect, malnutrition and out of reach thirst quenchers, to join many others on their zimmer frames and in mobility vehicles. In a combined effort they marched, drove and shuffled to prisons all over Britain, demanding permanent residence. After all, they had contributed to the wealth of the country, they felt it was their human right to share the secure environment and grand lifestyle they were denied.

After many successful con tricks over a ten-year period, Jaws Brown's ego and ambition got the better of him, and he planned and successfully executed the biggest con trick in history. He sold off a large quantity of Britain's gold reserves at a fraction of their value to investment Banks in Ireland and Iceland.

From the start he was a prime suspect and under police surveillance.

With no idea that the police net was closing in on him Brown was planning to move from his native town of Kirkcaldy after selling his residence, which did not belong to him, and caused Scotland Yard great anxiety. With the recession in full swing they could no longer afford to pay junior officers more than the Prime Minister earns in overtime pay, to keep track of Brown's devious scheming, night and day.

Ken Clark a former Chief Constable, who had been demoted for his reluctance to lock up criminals and falling asleep on the job, pleaded to be allowed to do this jaw yawning task on his basic salary, and pay his own expenses. He was desperate to atone for his past sins, including his former love affair with the Euro currency and to curry favour. His generous and unheard of offer was accepted.

Two days later Brown was in Kirkcaldy High Street, enjoying his favourite past time, 'Now you see it. Now you don't,' sleight of hand tricks on the gullible public. A friend warned him that a stranger with a posh English accent and slight stammer, unkempt appearance, Hush Puppy shoes, a paunch, and bags under his eyes was showing a mug shot of Brown to the public and asking, "Have you seen this man?"

In a bit of a panic Jaws Brown rushed back to his Mansion, which he had claimed under Squatter Rights and put up for sale, unfurnished, the day before. His main priority at the moment was a quick getaway from prying eyes. Packing his few belongings into his top of the range BMW (The bulk of his wardrobe was scattered in a number of safe houses in the Kingdom of Fife, in case of just such an emergency.) In his line of work you had to be prepared for any calamity, he drove the two miles to a flat situated in Forth Avenue, in a quiet street behind the railway station, glancing anxiously in his rear mirror in case he was being followed. George Osbourne, who lived at the flat was a close companion, who shared many of Brown's interests and hobbies. Although a very rich man, who could have mixed with the jet set, Osbourne preferred to keep a low profile.

Because of his reluctance to part with his money he was shunned by his neighbours.

This suited Brown, who was also aware that Osbourne knew when to keep his mouth shut. With his BMW safely out of sight in a corner of the railway station, he spent a pleasant evening with George discussing the dreadful state of the economy, and who was responsible. Osbourne was intrigued with Jaws Brown's risk taking lifestyle and what he had got away with. His visitor left at dawn the next morning, more than a little worried about the mysterious stranger who was stalking him. He made his way inland to his next refuge, on the outskirts of the town of Dunfermline, the birthplace of Andrew Carnegie, the town benefactor.

Isobella and Alec Sparring, with next door neighbour Jennie Rennie, a widow, lived in a quiet cul-de-sac. They were staunch, lifelong friends of Jaws Brown. He had spread much goodwill in the area, by giving away large sums of money for parents to open Bank accounts for newly born children. The Sparrings were a delightful and devoted couple who were generous to a fault. They sought no remuneration from Brown when he stayed with them. Their attitude to his lifestyle was that of Robin Hood, a legend to the people. Jennie Rennie on the other hand, got rushes of adrenaline when he let out angry outbursts of abuse against those that had let him down and betrayed his trust, on working trips south of the Scottish borders in England.

Brown sometimes stayed with her when he lay low to regain his senses after a bout of Boom or Bust excesses. Knowing his BMW would soon be traced he drove it to the town of Cowdenbeath, a few miles away. At a small back street garage he exchanged it for cash and a clapped out Mondeo, with no road tax or insurance, so he could blend in with the thousands of other illegal motorists and Crash for Cash insurance scammers. After a week he felt relaxed with a few drams of whisky and nightly chats on happier times, interspersed with political debate and how they could change the country for the better.

They all agreed it was no surprise that illegal immigrants were camped around the French coast as they had been doing for years, risking their necks to get into Britain. And why the bloody hell our mealy mouthed politicians had not taken the bull by the horns years ago by stopping the influx completely. That ethnic Brits had been treated as second class citizens for decades by multi racial obsessed governments ignoring the wishes of the electorate on most major issues. The biggest fear of them all was as they became an ethnic minority in their own country Middle East type chaos and bloodshed could be a future worry. As the debate got more heated the name of someone called Enoch Powell was mentioned.

A week later a dishevelled Englishman, with baggy eyes and a paunch was seen by Jennie, acting suspiciously near the statue of Carnegie in Dunfermline Glen. The next day wanted posters for Jaws Brown were on display all over the town. Brown was dejected; it was only a matter of time before he was spotted. Jennie, bless her, came to his rescue. She worked in a fancy dress shop and disguised him in a full length black shroud, with only slits for his eyes. Something like a common disguise seen all over Britain, although our dithering law makers were thinking of banning, and rightly so, hoods and masks on peaceful protest marches. Feeling secure and invisible in his new attire, even though it made it awkward to wear his spectacles, blow his nose or have a pee, he moved back to the East Coast and another safe house in the fishing community of Largo. His English shadow was beginning to irritate him. Who was he? And what was his aim?

Connie and her sister Shirley were Essex born and bred. With their combined brood of fifteen children all with different dads, they moved from Essex to Scotland. It was their only chance to better themselves and families. Being from a different country, England, and classed as immigrants, they were given luxury accommodation in a five star Hotel, and went to the top of the housing list. Three houses were then knocked into one under the supervision of Keith Jazz, head of the council 'Ask and get Housing Department.'

When settled in their new ten bedroom home with all mod cons, which they complained was a bit small, they sent for their parents, who were in their dotage and placed them in a free care home for the elderly. Connie's two eldest sons, Patel and Abromovich, and Shirley's teenage daughter, Kate, were soon enjoying a free education at St. Andrews University. Shirley hoped and prayed that Kate would meet a high flying young man from a wealthy and stable background. With their subsidised council rent, income support, child benefits and payments from ten wealthy, traceable dads, through the Child Support Agency plus the house being fully furnished by charitable organisations, the two ladies were fairly happy. A guest like Jaws Brown was always welcome. He was generous with his money, especially to the children, after all it had been tricked out of other people, and so parting with it was no big deal.

Uncle Jaw, as he was known to the family, was given a warm welcome as he thrust ten-pound notes into grasping hands, with a smug smile on his face. He was badly in need of some family comfort, after all he had been through. The children had an early tea of potato crisps, big macs with fries, twenty trays of assorted meals from Indian and Chinese takeaways, washed down by a flood of coke. They then retired to solitary confinement with their Computers and Ipod's in bedrooms and playrooms all over the house. The two unmarried mothers then left their guest in a relaxed mood with a large glass of his favourite tipple, a sixty-pounds-a-bottle of vintage malt whisky.

They then went into their luxurious extended kitchen. They were about to prepare themselves for dressing the 'Essex Sandwiches,' speciality of the house. The exotic ingredients were fresh and free from toxic preservatives. The secret recipe had been handed down through generations of Essex girls, making them a much sought after and talked about commodity. After a long evening of eating and drinking a jolly threesome staggered off to bed, a giggling Shirley clutching a Computer dongle dropped by one of the kids. A few days later the identity and Ken Clark's mission became clear, in the headlines of a local newspaper, complete with his photograph and Brown's.

A few days later stalker Ken was in the news again, being asked about his relentless chase of Scotland's most notorious conman, and for a conservative view on his crafty quarry. With a hasty goodbye to his hosts and their families and in a raging mood Jaws Brown took to the road again.

Hoping to cover his tracks among the golfers and tourists, he moved up to the East Coast to Jessie Mandelson's luxury bungalow in St. Andrews. He had reluctantly bypassed the picturesque fishing villages of Crail, St. Monans, Elie, Pittenween and Anstruther, all had taken a battering from their betrayal to the European Union's fishing fleets Armadas, by a British government. Jessie Mandelson was a divorcee from a civil marriage partner, Clair Shortcake. She was now a turncoat and Brown's part-time mistress and Banker. He had no faith in

High Street Banks who had been known to give customers bad service and get themselves into debt with client's money. Jessie supplemented her alimony by murky mortgagee deals, false insurance claims and handling stolen goods. It could be said she was a lady with a corrupt sense of adventure.

After three nights of pleasure with Jessie, a tired and frustrated Brown went on a bender. He got plastered on ten pints of bitter with whisky chasers. In a drunken rage he stared at the newspaper cutting of Ken Clark and stunned Jessie with a sudden uncontrollable outburst,

"It isnae fair Jessie that man Clark and the damned Polis are mackin ma life a bloody misery. That Clark's got it in fur me, mac nae mistake aboot that, the man is a bloody maniac," he screamed. With a pointed finger he jabbed Clark's photo in the throat screaming, "I hope you rot in hell damn you."

At that precise moment Ken Clark choked to death on a Spanish red herring, outside an Anstruther fish and chip shop. When the news and timing of Clark's demise reached him the shock changed his life. He swore on his mither's life to go straight.

He bought a house in Tayport with magnificent views across the river to Dundee, and gave the rest of his money to good causes. Jaws never pointed a finger again and became known as Tightfist. He made a living on the after- dinner circuit as a faceless speaker known only as the mystery man in the black shroud.

FACT

Gordon Brown became Prime Minister of Britain after allegedly making an agreement with his predecessor Tony Blair. The democratic process of electing a new leader of the Labour Party never took place. This could have led to the destruction of the parliamentary system and the downward spiral to dictatorship.

In the recession, which took hold in 2008, Brown announced in Parliament to howls of derision from the opposition, that by lending billions of pounds of taxpayers money to Banks who had gambled with customers and shareholders money, that he had 'Saved the World financially.'

The greed and arrogant behaviour of Bankers to those they put into debt, and are indebted to, is beyond belief. In a fair and equal society they would be denied by law of continuing with their obscene bonus culture and given mental health treatment for their addictive contempt of the general public.

The New Labour Party slogan, 'Things Can Only Get Better' was one word out of tune, 'Worse' for 'Better' would have struck the right note. Apart from the Billions lent to the Banks, New Labour, after an exemplary no more boom or bust start, later began spending money like there was no tomorrow, in a desperate effort to stay in power.

After his disastrous election defeat, aided by his true thoughts being broadcast accidentally to the public, Brown kept a low profile for a while. He then began lobbying to become the £270,000 a year head of the 'International Monetary Fund' to, as a spokesman was quoted, 'Stop the next financial crisis.' The Tory Party deputy chairman, Michael Fallon, no doubt astonished at Brown's brazen conceit, stated,

"Mr. Brown has yet to face up to the legacy of debt he

bequeathed to the taxpayers. This is a case of putting the arsonist in charge of the fire station."

The new Coalition Government brought about by disenchanted electorate of all parties is, sad to say, already up to its elbows in broken election promises they were elected on.

The British people are now seriously questioning the need for expenses riddled Parliament, packed with men and women full of broken promises and U-turns. They have led us ever deeper into the quagmire of the European Union, with broken promises of a Referendum. Or that other Institution, filled with ermine robed pensioners and known as the House of Lords, with questions asked for filling palms with silver.

Since the back stabbing of Margaret Thatcher by her own Conservative colleagues, the British way of life has been gradually eroded away. We are now ruled in nearly every sense of the word, by a bunch of overpaid, mindless and faceless European pen pushers and computer converts. Why did our elected leaders not make a belated stand when we were ordered not to import bent bananas? That, with all the other senseless rules and regulations, topped by human rights being judged by them, should have awakened our politicians to their speediest U-turn ever. Did any of them feel guilty over turning their backs on the British Commonwealth? I doubt it, or making criminals out of honest British tradesmen, for weighing produce in our traditional pounds and ounces. They were responsible for the death of one tradesman who died from the stress of persecution, from their cowardly acceptance of all things, European Union.

One of my greatest delights in life is to listen to imported American television programmes. The greatest and largest English speaking country in the World still speaks and acts non metric. The Americans have a greater respect for our heritage and way of life than our elected rabble; who have discarded our British rights to the dustbin.

The American attitude should make those who betrayed the

British way of life, which was fought and sacrificed for through two World Wars, hang their heads in shame.

Expense scandals at the heart of power, of bribery and corruption questions asked of forces of the law. Hacking phones by newspapers to the darkest depths, all three in connection left the public in distress.

Referendums promised then arrogantly refused, by oily tongues that slickly turn in upon themselves.

If only they had listened to the voter's point of view, who sensed what was coming long before we knew, we would not all now be drowning in a bureaucratic Euro stew.

BRITAIN
2025

There was something eerily beautiful about the moon in winter as its light streaked through the trees, leaving large dark shadows. These were perfect cover for Jags Prescott as he waited impatiently in Sari Park on the outskirts of the multi racial city of Leicester. It was the year 2025, like all retired people over the age of seventy-five part time working was compulsory. In the earlier years of the century, public confidence and patience with the three main political parties had finally run out. The native born population angry at the way their wishes had long been ignored in favour of foreigners, who had put nothing into the national coffers, revolted. A bloodless revolution took place.

The nation was now run by an All Party Senate. Members were elected from all sections of the community by regional votes, for a three-year period on a fixed income. Anyone found fiddling the taxpayers was sentenced to ten years hard labour with no remission. All major decisions were decided by a National Referendum through the Internet. Human Rights law only applied to law-abiding citizens, anyone making unjust or stupid claims were fined and publicly humiliated. The dinosaur of political correctness was abolished. Voting on state affairs became compulsory from the age of sixteen. The House of Commons and the House of Lords plus Buckingham Palace, rid of all their wealthy trappings, became hard labour prisons for those serving a life sentence.

The All Party Senate served the nation from a derelict warehouse in Bradford, tastefully decorated with bankrupt stock wallpaper. Within a year of the revolution the old and infirm were released from imprisonment in their own homes and could walk the streets without the fear of attack. Muggers and young thugs didn't take kindly to the death sentence for attacking the vulnerable. Burglary became a thing of the past when life imprisonment with no remission and hard labour became law.

Prescott long since retired, had been assigned to the Public Offenders Council Section. As he shivered in the cold night air he could not help envying his buddy, Tony Blair, who was studying the art of confidence tricksters and coral density in Australia, with his wife, after retiring to the sun. With only squirrels for company he scanned the car park and bottle bank area twenty yards form his vantagepoint, his Byers van was safely hidden in some bushes. He thought back to the times of government incompetence and neglect of the law-abiding majority in favour of criminals and their do-gooder allies. Of Judges in a state of senility, way out of touch with reality. Industrial Tribunals for the working classes, chaired by people who acted like prosecutors with a demeaning attitude to claimants.

A figure appeared on the far side of the park. It was nearing curfew time for the under sixteen's. The youth relieved himself then zipped up his flies. Prescott clenched his fist in anger but let the offence go unpunished, hoping some dog owner had taken a chance on his or her liberty and left some dog pooh for the lad to tread in. He was on surveillance for a set purpose, to apprehend or report a sighting of a criminal who had been a menace to the Senate for many years. Section helpers were on watch in prime target areas of the city, after intelligence reports of this public enemy number one. Crime had increased from zero to one third of a hundred per cent over the last five years. Maybe it was time for a Referendum on stiffer sentences.

As he scanned the area behind him with powerful night sights, supplied for this job, he saw movements in the darkening shadows. He gave way to a moment of panic, there were strange, wild creatures on the loose all over the country. Three of these inter breeds had been around for a long time, nibbling away at the country's wealth, undetected by most of the population, the Labourastrikeforus, Liberalelhomo and Toriaboris were as great a danger to themselves as the rest of the country. When cornered, their snapping, back biting and infighting was stomach churning. In the year 2006 Animal Rights activists had freed thousands of animals all over the country.

Large numbers of these laboratory experiments had survived in the wild. Over the years they interbred into bizarre and sometimes dangerous life forms. The government of the time did not help by banning Fox hunting, making them more or less an endangered species. The Fox population grew out of control and interbred with, among others, vicious Alsations, released on striking miners by their angry police handlers. Racing Whippets who their striking owners could not afford to feed during the violent, Thatch Head Scargill era of the late nineteen hundreds, when the whole country was undermined. This led to the existence of a fearsome hybrid named the Alwhipafox. The creature was agile, cunning and savage, with an acquired taste for human flesh.

As they hunted in packs from dusk till dawn, Jags Prescott had good reason to be concerned. A part time government busybody and sleep inducer, credited as the creator of the Brazil Wax, unselfishly gave his all to try and exterminate the Alwhipafox. Professor Mandelson took out second mortgages on his homes to finance research into the production of a sleeping sickness drug, which at one stage nearly succeeded in wiping out the Alwhipafox. The survivors, due to their devious nature made a remarkable comeback against all the odds, they became a law unto themselves.

With the demise of the railways after a permanent strike by angry and disgruntled passengers, the Alwhipafox foraged from their railway sleeper dens and abandoned sidings at will, with all the other hybrids including the giant headed Mink Skinner Otter, a human induced catastrophe. The railways had been replaced by inter city robot driven carriages named Byers, after the man responsible for their manufacture. Powered by magnetic propulsion on a single rail, they were pollution free and easily accessible from magnetic propelled pavements and broadwalks. With the decrease in the use of petrol and diesel driven vehicles, two lanes of all motorways were re-turfed as re-claimed green belt. A green belt stake rush ensued, led by itinerant travellers.

The caravan swelling population increased by the thousands overnight. Councils went into the red as millions of pounds were lost in council tax and the housing market collapsed. Ministers faced a House of Commons enquiry and had their hands slapped.

As he kept his lonely vigil Prescott thought of the state of lawlessness and mass immigration that had taken place before the Revolution. As the thin blue line of law and order dispersed in large numbers to the coasts, to repel the swarms of illegal immigrants, law and order was in a traffic jam. Sari Park became a squatter camp for thugs, drug dealers and joy riders. Cars stolen by kids as young as ten were set on fire for the sheer hell of it. The area had also fostered its fair share of teenage unmarried mothers, chain smoking impatiently during their career move, a top of the list three bedroomed council house. Smoking the weed was now a criminal offence, under age addicts served six months in a tented boot camp on a stable diet of cold turkey. If they re-offended they faced three years in prison with their parents, and repeated showings of television's Big Brother as their only entertainment.

Hard drugs were prohibited unless on prescription, illegal drug use meant life imprisonment. Drug dealers were not so lucky, they served two years as guinea pigs in a scientific experimental unit. If they survived they could look forward to death by lethal injection. Prescription drugs were only obtainable from Senate hospitals, patrolled by armed guards. Parental centres housed neighbours from hell where they were taught basic morals and sterilised. The old fashioned ideology that children should be seen and not heard made a startling comeback.

The opening of non-profit Senate shops in towns and villages had reversed shopping trends. The out of town supermarkets could no longer compete and leased their premises to the Senate, who turned them into Litter Lout centres and Inter Space holiday departure and arrival points. Litter offenders spent eight hours a day for a week on pick it up bin it, drop it, bin it, courses, knee high in an acre of the now banned junk mail and plastic bags.

Second offenders were sent to land fill rubbish sites on three months dig it up, re-bury it digs. There was no third time offender on record. The countryside also benefited from a minimum sentence of ten years for illegal dumping of rubbish. Most of the prisons had been closed because for some reason people didn't seem to want to go there anymore.

The Moon was now home to a gigantic domed holiday complex, devoid of time-share reps. It was built as a replica to all the tiny parts of life over the last hundred years that were actually pleasant in between the almost continuous wars, torture, starvation and suffering of the world's vast majority. The old fashioned holidays with knees in the chest flying had taken a back seat. The huge Inter Space Rockets had full-length reclining seats, with walkabouts for star and space viewing, plus all modern facilities for three hundred passengers. They were powered by a weightless fuel named Trolly Titanium, which was invented by Neil Kincockup who awoke one morning with his head in a spin. After much trial and error it was eventually refined in Iran and renamed National Hell Supplement, or N.H.S. for short. Inter Space holidays were on a rota basis, anyone with a criminal or dubious terrorist record was banned from travelling anywhere for life.

An owl startled Jags Prescott out of his dream holiday mood as it swooped on its prey near the Park playing field; he stamped his feet as the cold began to bite into his Chinese boots and clothing.

Three super powers now existed, their currency now known as the Yankee Obama, the Chinese Triad and last but not least the Indian In-Got. Euroland could not compete with each giant expanding economy and was swallowed up. With a new found freedom to travel a flood of Chinese made their way to enter easy Britain. Their destination was France, to enjoy a massive baby boom outside their strict birth control homeland, a refined health service, large pensions and the freedom to strike or disrupt without the fear of prosecution. France in desperation dynamited their end of the Channel Tunnel to stem the flow of illegal Chinese and others from Britain.

France cut its Human Rights law to the bone as their treasury was raided by frivolous complaints from the illegal and criminals. In fear of complete domination by China and fearful of American friendly fire, Euroland became, with England, a part of the United States of India. Scotland and Wales remained Independent, as they had been for many years. Before gaining full Independence from England, the Scottish Parliament reversed or changed many decisions made by the British Parliament in London, which strange as it may seem, was led by a group of Scots. When the Scottish Parliament introduced free university education, improved and cheaper care for their elderly plus many other benefits, people in England became a little upset.

Many poor and middle class white English and Muslims made a permanent move to Scotland. Their glowing reports of life in the north attracted so many more in the south that the Scots were forced into rebuilding the whole of the Roman Empire's Hadrian's Wall to keep them out. Scotland finally gained full Independence under the banner of the Scottish National and Muslim Party. Meanwhile in the south, English parents were sending their daughters to Bollywood dancing classes in the hope that they would catch the eye, in their perma-tan and sari, of a rich man with marriage in mind. With their lower birth rate and mixed marriages the white English population was now a minority.

In Wales a Welsh child singer had progressed into a television personality and from that into politics. She became the first female Prime Minister of her country. A song was written in her honour, with the title 'Rugby, Bubbly and Church,' it was sung to the tune of 'Land of My Father's.' The first law passed under the leadership of Prime Minister Church stated that no foreigner would be allowed to buy property in Wales or stay for more than six weeks, apart from Welsh exiles with holiday homes.

Wales became the last country in the whole of Europe to be ruled wholly by its own nationals. America had taken it for granted that England, their closest ally, would eventually join them as another state.

This dream was destroyed by the collapse of the American housing market in 2008. This caused a chain reaction around the world bringing untold hardship and misery. A case of friendly fire from greedy Bankers. America's reluctance to lead from the front in the fight against Global Warming had also done nothing to enhance its reputation. It was shaken out of its complacency a few years later. A Chinese corporation succeeded in a take over bid for America's worldwide food suppliers. Macdonald's, Beef Burger King and Kentucky Fried Chicken were dissolved into the 'Melting Pots'. This was after obesity had spread around the globe like a cancer and people were dying in there thousands from gas inhalation. The 'Melting Pots' served a variety of quality foods and their chopsticks gave their customers some much-needed exercise. Their most popular dishes were 'Doodle While You Noodle', Doodle While You Dunk', 'Chopstick Duet', 'Yankee Doodle Jammy', 'Dragon Fire My Bite', 'Milk Rattle And Roll', and the chef's surprise 'Text Till You Retch'.

The 'Melting Pots' restaurants come kindergartens became national institutions teaching racial harmony, respect and protection for all life forms and the environment, with their pleasantly illustrated and anti blasphemous Doodle books.

Jags Prescott was startled from his thoughts by the mournful sound of a siren from the vicinity of Mandela Park, on the other side of the city. Like many others he had been amazed that a man, who spent the best part of his life in a cell, should have a Park named after him that sat in the shadow of the towering wall of the city prison. The hair on the back of his bloated neck stiffened in alarm as he spotted a frail, stooped figure at the entrance to the Park, checking it out for what seemed like an eternity, before entering. With a shuffling gait the figure moved across the car park toward the bottle bank, which had four holes for different coloured bottles. To his astonishment Prescott saw that the figure was carrying, with difficulty, three supermarket plastic bags, banned nearly two decades ago because of the damage caused to wildlife and the environment.

The bags were filled to the brim and the shadowy figure reached the bottle bank with a weary sigh. Prescott pressed his microchip button to alert headquarters, before moving in for the kill. This person was committing what had been in the crazy days of political correctness, the nation's most loathed crime, putting coloured bottles in the clear bottle hole. Even now this act caused great confusion and anger when the multi racial council workers opened the banks. The mixing of glass had also become the international symbol for the right to express one's thoughts freely without being accused of racism.

Prescott crept up on the suspect and challenged it. The figure turned slowly towards him. He felt weak at the knees when he saw whom he was about to arrest. It was none other than public enemy number one, Majestic Thatcher. When he regained his composure he helped the tottering Majestic to his hidden Byer's van, with the little respect he could muster. With his prisoner safely in the van, his chest swelled with pride as he thought of the rewards and publicity he would get from his arrest.

Reality hit him like a hammer blow, behind him he heard a savage snarling that tailed off into a whippet-like whine, which chilled him to the marrow. With his bodily functions running out of control he turned to face the pointed fangs of the Alwhipafox.

Prescott's last shift was nearly over.

MADEIRA
2011

The manuscript for this book was completed on the Portuguese Island of Madeira, tourist destination for people from many countries and all walks of life. If you have ever visited this Island I am sure you will agree it is worthy of a mention.

From approaching the Island by air on to the short landing strip, which extends out to sea supported on concrete pillars, with a background of towering mountains, this is a splendid holiday destination. The moderate climate, encouraged by the steep rise in altitude, to the rain producing clouds hovering over the mountains, produces an amazing variety of plants, flowers and tropical fruits. Vegetables from the humble potato to sweet corn abound. Many of these crops grow on a series of steps cut into the very edge of the mountain sides, as Louie, my Jeep Safari driver said,

"You could finish up well mashed stretching for that last potato."

High up in the mountains it is strange to see cows, wandering about as they graze on narrow tracks bordered by sheer drops, with not a farm or house in sight. I was informed that most of the mountain people keep a family cow for their own personal needs. Each cow has its own private accommodation of a small shed.

The Laveda walks range from flat and easy to a bit of a challenge for the more energetic.

Down in the coastal areas there are water sports to suit most tastes, or you might fancy a boat trip to view Dolphins and Whales. If you fancy sunbathing on the deck of a large Catamaran, the pleasure is yours for the taking.

There is also changes of scenery to enjoy, from the natural pools formed in volcanic rock, in the sea at Port Moniz, and the still working fishing village of Camara-De-Lobos to name but two.

Overlooking the village and harbour is the Sir Winston Churchill bar, built on the site where he sat to practice his artistic skills, on the surrounding area.

As most of the population lives in the busy capital of Funchia, there is an abundance of small restaurants around the Cable Car station in the old town. The Cable ride takes you up to Monte Gardens and the Botanical Gardens. If you like a thrill on the way down, the Toboggan run awaits. The sledges, with two men in attendance, speed down a smooth worn tarmac road, which seems never ending.

The Casino with top class entertainment lies just out of town, in the Lido area. Farther along this road is the Centro Commercial, Eden Mar shopping centre. Most of the nightly entertainment, a cluster of hotels, restaurants, and shops are in this area. The Four Views Hotel, opposite the shopping centre provides a variety of nightly entertainments. The local folklore dancers and musicians on Friday nights are especially entertaining.

The Hole In The Wall bar and Obrions are opposite each other next to the main street. During the day and evening you can relax in the courtyards with a drink and a meal. On Friday and Saturday nights you can join the locals from 10.30p.m. until 2a.m. as they let their hair down. The group of musicians in Obrions are very versatile. From slow tempo Jazz they gradually warm up into modern melodies and Rock and Roll as the night progresses. The lead singer and keyboard player looks like a larger version of Bob Geldoff, without the wrinkles. He has a great voice and a vibrant personality.

There is a great choice of food available. On the expensive side try a steak on stone. This arrives raw and cooks to your liking, something similar to an Indian sizzler, or the local

Scabbard fish, which tastes I think, like a mixture of Cod and Haddock, prices vary. For a cheap filling meal try one of the nine different fillings in a Venezuela speciality called a Cachapas at the Multi Delicious, Autentico Palador Latino. It looks like a pancake or omelette but is actually sweet corn baked with no oil. Ingredients include powdered milk, eggs and vanilla essence.

As you walk down to the Eden Mar shopping centre, past the Gorhuliho Hotel the Indian Bombay restaurant beckons. Farther along on the top floor hidden in the corner of its large terrace is the Barracuda bar. The family run bar of Dino, Luisa Joanee and Pedro give a warm welcome, and a range of meals at a reasonable price. Try a special like chicken piri piri, or beef stew.

If you never make it to this Island I hope you have gained some enjoyment from my experiences.

P.S. No holiday would be complete without a little moan. Are there too many taxis in Funchia? To the taxi drivers in the Monte area? 'Come on guys, a smiling face and some cheery banter with the tourists waiting on the regular bus service would, I am sure, gain you many a fare deal.'

VICTIMIZATION OF THE INNOCENT
THE BEGINNING OF THE END

After decades of soft authority, with discipline abandoned, the breakdown of British society and culture, shows no sign of slowing down. Human Rights appears to be in favour of those with criminal intent, while victims of injustice are treated with contempt. The State has tied the hands of those who should control, the cotton wool wrapped generation who crass and brass now act. Honest, stealth taxed citizens who for this country fought and slaved, are at the back of queue, for everything, this Welfare State was made.

DISCIPLINE
(BRITISH STYLE)

Ten-year-olds murdered
A little lad of two
Educated and pampered
Now in secret live as free.
Other kids running wild
Smoke, drink, sniff pots of glue.
Extortion by the bully
Now out of control
Of innocent heads, suicide roll call.
Elders live in fear and stress
Of the child they once held dear.
Threaten to smack a child of yours
Of social services beware.
The days have long gone
When punishment fitted the crime
And law and order was respected.

YOB AND STEAL SOCIETY
2011

Roll the joint, smoke the dope
Wrap my brains in overcoat
Drink the booze, lose control
Temper hits danger zone
Go on ecstasy, in a daze
Slavery from my own free will.
Take joy ride in someone's car
No tax, insurance, what a laugh
Three best mates died in crash.
Six of us on to one
Put the boot in, play the thug
Grannies cower when they see us…
On a gang bang, hold the bird down
She asked for it, out late at night.
Scratch cars, set fire to schools
Break into property, then we trash
Steal anything on order sheet
Buyer waits with wad in fist.
We've taken over, we now rule
Parents now under our control.
If not show us enough respect
Bullet or Shaftin, you will get.